DEAD WIDOW ROAD

THE HORRORS OF SOBOLTON BOOK THREE

AMY CROSS

CONTENTS

DEAD
WIDOW
ROAD

CHAPTER ONE

Today...

"BABY YOU'RE THE ONE, you're the light of my life. You're the girl of my dreams I wanna make you my wife. Ooh-ah, ooh-ah, ooh-ah badda-boom! Yeah!"

Drumming his fingertips against the top of the steering wheel, Doctor Robert Law couldn't help singing along to the song as he drove. He was having to keep his speed low to navigate the twisting, icy roads leading back to Sobolton; having taken his monthly trip for an evening meal at a favorite restaurant out of town, he was making his way home with only the radio for company, and that was just the way he liked things. Having always been a somewhat solitary man, and a confirmed bachelor, Robert was even bopping slightly in his seat as he felt the beat of the music flowing through his body.

"Girl you make me wanna do bad things," he sang loudly, accompanying the song as it reached its crescendo. "Girl you make me wanna blow the doors of this thing! Gadda-go!"

As snow fell down, picked out by the car's headlights, Robert steered the vehicle around the next corner. He knew these roads like the back of his hand; better, even, since he'd been driving in the area around Sobolton almost all his life. He felt completely at ease, almost at one with the car, and as he took a tight left-hander with slightly too much speed – for the conditions, at least – he paid no care as he felt the tires slipping slightly. He knew he was in total control of the vehicle, and he knew -

"Girl, you're a whole lot of -"

Suddenly he spotted a figure ahead, standing in the middle of the road. Startled, he barely had time to slam his foot on the brake pedal before turning the wheel, spinning the car around until it bumped to a halt just a few feet from the solitary person who apparently had no idea that standing in the road might be a dangerous move.

"What the -"

After taking a moment to get his breath back, Robert peered out at the figure. He could just about tell that it was a woman, wearing a long dark dress and with some kind of shawl over her head, perhaps even a veil covering her face. She was standing in the snow, apparently oblivious to the icy conditions, and she appeared to be focused entirely on the space beyond the road's far side, where an old guardrail marked the start of a precipitous drop into the river below.

"What the..."

With his mouth hanging open, Robert continued to stare at the figure for a few more seconds before switching the car's engine off. His heart was racing, and as he opened the door and climbed out – taking a moment to grab his walking stick – he began to wonder whether he'd almost run straight into a complete lunatic.

"What... the...?"

He waited, but she showed no sign of a reaction at all.

"What are you doing there?" he called out, holding onto the car door in case his feet slipped on the ice. "Are you crazy? I almost ran you straight over!"

The figure turned to him, and despite the dark veil over its face, Robert let out a sigh as he realized that he recognized her after all.

"Susan?" he continued. "Susan Walpole, what are you doing out here so late at night? You're gonna catch your death of cold!"

"I had to come," she replied, her voice sounding a little frail. "I just... I had to. It's only on nights like these that I can properly hear them."

"Hear who?" he asked incredulously, already wondering whether this usually sensible woman had suffered some kind of brain injury. "Susan, you're in the middle of the road!" He waited, but she still somehow seemed completely unaware that this was a problem. "Susan, have you lost your mind? I'm being serious here, what if I'd hit you?"

"I have to try to hear them again," she said, before slowly turning and looking over at the guardrail. "I'm the only one left, Robert. If I don't do something, who will?"

"Well..."

He hesitated, but deep down he already knew what she meant. Staring at the guardrail, he could almost hear the cries and screams echoing through the years; he remembered that day so very well, and he knew that in some ways the pain and horror had never quite left his sleepy little hometown. After a moment – against his better judgment – he let go of the car door and carefully picked his way across the ice until he reached the guardrail, and then he looked down at the darkness far below.

"I hear them sometimes, Robert," Susan continued. "I always have. They're still down there."

***

"Daddy, can I be excused to go and fetch some of my toys to show John?"

"Did you finish your meal?" Tommy asked, craning his neck to get a better look at Josh's dinner plate. "Well, it looks like you did. You can go if your mother says it's alright."

"Mom?"

"Go on, then," Tracy sighed, smiling as she watched her son clambering off his chair and racing out of the dining room. "Sorry, John," she added, turning to their guest, "but Josh really seems to have taken a liking to you."

"That's fine," John replied, feeling distinctly out of place as he sat at the far end of the table. "He's a sweet kid. He's a credit to you both."

"I don't think I asked," Tracy said, as she got to her feet and began to gather the dirty plates. "Do you have any children, John?"

"Uh..."

For a moment John hesitated, not really knowing what to say.

"A son," he managed finally, "but... he lives a long way from here."

"Oh? Is he abroad?"

"No, he's... in the country," John continued, already wondering whether he should have lied. "I don't see him that often. He's a long way from here."

"Is he going to come visit you soon?"

"I really don't know."

"Sorry, I shouldn't pepper you with questions," she admitted as she carried the plates toward the kitchen. "I guess I just can't help the fact that I'm a little nosy. Tommy'll tell you how often that gets me into trouble, I should know better by now but I guess it's just something that's part of me."

As she disappeared into the kitchen, John and Tommy were left sitting in awkward silence at either end of the dinner table. John knew he should say something to his host, but in truth he was feeling distinctly uncomfortable and he was already wishing that he'd postponed the night altogether; the invitation had been weighing on him for a few days, and he'd decided to simply rip the band-aid off and hope for the best, but deep down he knew he'd never been the dinner party type. As far as he was concerned, small-talk was a foreign language.

"Did you like the food?" Tommy asked finally, clearly keen to get the conversation flowing again.

"Wonderful, thank you," John replied, forcing a smile. "Your wife's a very good cook."

"I did the pastry," Tommy explained. "I'm not a great cook, but for some reason I'm really good at pastry. Tracy calls me a pastry whisperer sometimes, which I don't mind. I don't know where I got the skill from, it just seems to be something I'm naturally good at."

"She's a very nice woman."

"I hope so! I'm married to her!"

The silence returned, and John was now wondering whether he could make another trip to the bathroom. He'd gone twice already since arriving a couple of hours earlier, just to gain a little respite from the otherwise stifling atmosphere, and part of him worried that he seemed like he had a bladder problem. He glanced around the dining room, wondering when Tracy would return and save thcm both, but he could hear her pottering around in the kitchen so he figured she'd be a while; he could also hear Josh bumping around in a room upstairs, and he had to admit that even the young boy's return would be a blessing in that moment. No matter what else he tried, he'd already come to accept that he and Tommy simply didn't have much to talk about besides work.

Which was fine, if they were at work. But if they were in a social situation... not so much.

"So how's Sobolton treating you?" Tommy asked finally, clearly running out of things to say. "You've been here... what, three weeks now? Are you liking the place?"

"Sure," John replied, even if that wasn't entirely true just yet. "It's certainly got an... interesting vibe."

CHAPTER TWO

Twenty years earlier...

"SO HE'S GOING TO be fine, as long as he keeps resting that leg," Lisa said as she helped Gary Dufresne carry his dog Wilbur out to the car in a sling. "The most important thing is that he doesn't get to the stitches, which he won't be able to do so long as he's wearing the cone."

"The cone of shame," Gary chuckled, taking a moment to adjust his grip before setting Wilbur down on the back seat. "There you go," he continued. "Man, he's not happy about wearing that thing. I've got a feeling he's gonna make my life hell for the next week."

"Try ten days," Lisa replied as she took a

step back. "It was quite a big operation, so the recovery time won't be quick."

Spotting movement across the road, she looked over toward the diner and saw a dozen people gathered in front of the small memorial near the diner. She raised a hand to shield her eyes from the sun; squinting as snow continued to fall, she watched as a woman stepped toward the memorial and knelt to set down a wreath.

"Huh," she continued. "Is it that time of year again?"

"May they rest in peace," Gary murmured.

For a few seconds they stood in silence, watching the ceremony. Lisa had seen the annual ritual many times in the past, but it always sent a chill through her bones. The worst part was seeing the assembled mourners and realizing that year by year their number dwindled a little more; two decades had gone past since the tragedy out at Henge Cliff, and while plenty of people in Sobolton still remembered that day so well, Lisa figured that one day that would change. Eventually there'd be no-one alive who'd experienced the tragedy, and then what would happen to the memorial ceremony? She couldn't help but wonder whether it would die out completely.

"You know," Gary said after a moment, "I

even hate driving past that place."

She turned to him.

"Henge Cliff, I mean," he continued. "Is it crazy that I kinda get the willies out there? Even in broad daylight, I don't like the place. Sometimes I drive the long way round, just to avoid it."

"I know the feeling," she replied.

"This town has certainly seen its fair share of sorrow over the years," Gary said as he slammed the door and made his way around to the other side of the car. "Don't you think we're about due a period of peace and quiet?"

"I think everyone'd like that," Lisa admitted, unable to stop watching as the ceremony continued.

"I mean, look at the place," Gary said. "Sobolton's not a huge town, it's not near anywhere important. People here just like to get on with their lives and be left alone." Pausing, he furrowed his brow for a moment. "Do you think every small town in America's like Sobolton?" he asked. "They can't be, can they? They can't have so many weird things happening, it's just impossible. Sobolton's a little... unusual in that respect, isn't it?"

"Definitely," she replied, before turning to him. "Listen, I should get going, but remember to let me know if the stitches on Wilbur's side look at all red or swollen. I'd rather deal with any problems early. If you leave these things, they only get worse over time."

***

"And one of those cookies, please," Lisa said a short time later, standing at the counter in the diner and looking at the offerings in a nearby display unit. "The ones with the pink icing?"

"Incredible," Wendy replied with a grin as she grabbed a pair of tongs.

"What do you mean?"

"Just that you're so like your father, it's unreal," Wendy continued, opening the back of the display. "We used to stock these exact cookies when I first worked here, and your father loved them. Then the factory burned down and we couldn't get them for years and years, until they came back into production a few months ago. Of course, your dad didn't live to see that day, but here you are asking for the exact same cookie."

"Huh," Lisa replied, trying to hide the fact that she felt a little uncomfortable. "That's... odd."

She watched as Wendy moved the tongs toward the cookie she'd requested.

"Actually," she said suddenly, "can I go for the blue one instead?"

"Are you sure?" Wendy asked.

"I changed my mind."

"Not the pink one?"

"No, not the pink one," Lisa continued, and now she was wishing she'd never even looked at the cookies. In fact, she was starting to wonder whether she should have ventured into the diner at all. "The blue one."

"Your dad never went for the blue ones," Wendy replied, taking one of the blue cookies out from the unit. "I remember him telling me one day that he'd tried a blue one and hated it. He was a man of his habits, wasn't he?"

"Apparently so," Lisa said through gritted teeth.

She watched as Wendy finished make her coffee, and then – hearing the diner's front door open – she turned just in time to see some of the mourners from outside making their way inside. As well as a few local dignitaries, including Sheriff Joe Hicks, she spotted three women wearing black, and she knew that these were the three surviving widows from the awful accident many years earlier. She watched as they made their way around the corner, and then she glanced out the window and spotted a fresh wreath next to the memorial.

"Great," Wendy whispered, keeping her

voice low as she set the coffee and cookie down in front of Lisa. "I know I shouldn't say this, but I never like it when they come in after the ceremony."

"It's only once a year," Lisa pointed out as she handed her some money.

"I know, but they sit there for hours," Wendy continued. "Like, I get it, what happened was tragic. But it's been twenty years now, do we really have to see the entire town come to a standstill just to remember the time a bus drove off the road? At least there are only three of the widows left now. I'm going to sound like a total stone-cold bitch for saying this, but I'll be glad when there are none of them left. At least then we won't all have to keep remembering bad things that happened years and years ago."

"I'm sure it'll be fine," Lisa murmured, surprised by Wendy's slightly callous tone.

"It's alright for you," Wendy replied, passing some change over, "you're not going to have them sitting around near you for the rest of the day. It's the same every year, they talk about what happened endlessly, repeating themselves over and over again." She let out a heavy sigh. "I know I sound bad, but it's just relentless. This one day each year is enough to make me lose my mind. Why can't they go to a bar and get drunk like normal people?"

"Maybe because they still don't have closure?" Lisa suggested. "After all, no-one ever worked out exactly what caused the crash."

"Sure, but just... get over it, already," Wendy added. "It's not like anyone can bring them back. If you ask me, sometimes the past is better left in the past. There's no benefit in constantly digging things up and never just letting it rest. Focus on what's going on now, because at the end of the day, that's all that matters." She paused, before sliding the coffee and cookie across the counter. "Enjoy your blue treat. Let me know what you think of it."

"Thanks," Lisa replied, taking her order and heading toward the door, only to slow a little as she saw the mourners taking their seats at the far end of the diner.

For a moment she felt a shiver run through her bones. She remembered her father talking about the tragedy of 1984, about how ten good Sobolton men had lost their lives in a tragedy that had never been explained; she remembered all the hushed gossip, all the rumors, all the arguments that had erupted as people had tried to guess what had caused the accident. Aside from the deaths in the crash, other lives had been ruined as well, and even two decades later battle-lines remained drawn between those who believed one theory and those who favored another. The terrible crash at Henge Cliff had left a scar across the town that had never healed.

"This whole town needs a cone," Lisa muttered under her breath, before opening the door and stepping outside, then stopping for a moment to take a deep breath of fresh wintry air. "Then again, maybe some scars *never* heal."

CHAPTER THREE

Today...

"OKAY, JUST SIT DOWN for a minute," Robert said as he shut the door to his house. "The heating's on, but I can turn it up a bit."

"You don't need to do that," Susan replied, stepping across the hallway before turning to him. "I shouldn't be here," she added, as if suddenly struck by a sense of panic. "Robert, I need to get back out there and keep listening."

"You could have died tonight," he pointed out.

"Nonsense."

"It's not nonsense," he continued. "You were standing in the middle of an icy road in the middle of winter, during some of the worst weather this town has seen in a century! Do you have any idea how dangerous your actions have been tonight?"

"And do *you* have any idea how desperate I am?" she asked.

"Susan..."

"Doris Warner died," she told him.

"I know. I heard."

"So that makes me the only one who's left," she pointed out, taking a step toward him. "Ten women lost their husbands in that crash, Robert. Over the forty years since that day, the other nine have died and now I'm the only one. Do you think it's a coincidence that, as time goes by, I'm also the only one who hears their voices?"

"What voices?"

"The voices of those poor men," she continued. "They call out to me. Sometimes I even hear them when I'm at home, when I'm in bed." She paused again, with tears in her eyes. "I hear all of them, at least I think I do, but it's my dear Timothy I hear the most. His soul is still out there, Robert, and he can't rest until the truth has come out about what really happened. You know it's been covered up, you know someone has been hiding things. If I don't find a way to listen to those voices, and to act on whatever they're trying to tell me, the truth might stay buried forever."

Robert opened his mouth to reply, before turning and making his way over to the liquor cabinet in the corner of the room.

"Whiskey?" he suggested.

"I don't drink," she replied. "I'm surprised you don't remember that."

"I remember," he said as he poured himself a drink. "I just thought over the years..."

His voice trailed off.

"I suppose I just thought," he continued, "that over the years you might have been... driven to it."

"By grief?" she suggested. "By sorrow? Rage? Regret? Perhaps I would have been if I'd been able to pick just one of those emotions, but instead I felt them all and more besides. The truth is, if I'd started drinking back then, I'd be dead from alcohol poisoning by now." She let out another heavy sigh. "Perhaps that would be for the best. Does anyone really want a silly old woman running round, trying to rake over the past? Isn't it maybe better if it's just left as a mystery?"

Robert hesitated, before taking a sip of whiskey. He thought for a moment, and already an idea was forming in his mind.

"Joe Hicks isn't the sheriff round these parts

now," he pointed out finally. "A new guy took over a few weeks ago. I know him a little, he's a good man. He might be able to help out with things that Joe Hicks couldn't." He paused again. "Or wouldn't."

***

"Are you okay in here?"

Surprised, John turned to see that Tracy had made her way through into the kitchen, where John had spent some time looking out the window after fetching a glass of water.

"Oh, I'm fine," he murmured, making his way over, "I was just -"

"Spending ten minutes in the kitchen," she replied with a faint, knowing smile. "I'm sorry if Josh overwhelmed you, he can be a little excitable. He's not too good at understanding social boundaries."

"No, that's fine," John said. "I just -"

"You look so uncomfortable," she added, cutting him off.

"I do?"

"Tommy's noticed it too," she continued. "We're not blind. You're not really a dinner party kind of guy, are you?"

"I'm very grateful to you for inviting me over," John replied, worried that he'd caused offense, "and for the lovely food and -"

Before he could finish, Tracy started laughing.

"What?" he asked, confused by her response. "What's wrong?"

"Nothing," she replied, shaking her head. "It's just that you're saying all the right things, which is very sweet. But none of that changes the fact that you look like you'd rather by anywhere else tonight. And before you apologize yet again, let me reassure you that you haven't been rude and we haven't taken it personally. In some ways, it's actually refreshing to meet someone who's so bad at lying."

"I don't really know what to say next," John admitted.

"Then don't say anything at all," she said, smiling as she placed a hand on the side of his arm. "I'm just sorry that you've wasted several hours this evening, trying to do something you probably knew was impossible. I might be reading too much into the situation, but I'm getting the feeling that you don't have a huge amount of experience with the traditional family unit kind of set-up."

"It's... complicated," John replied.

"Life usually is," she pointed out. "Listen, Tommy and I really enjoy having you over, but we also don't want you to feel uncomfortable. So why don't you stay for dessert, and then remember that you can leave at any point, and no-one will be offended."

"That's very kind of you."

"I'm used to dealing with awkward men," she said as she led him through to the front room. "You've met my husband, right? And my son."

"I've really enjoyed your hospitality this evening," John told her, still trying to find a few polite things to say. "Your son's a very smart young man, he's clearly been raised very well. He's a credit to you and Tommy."

"He has certain challenges," she admitted as they stopped at the window and looked out at the snow-covered garden, where Josh was throwing snowballs at a wall while Tommy watched and laughed. "One thing you're going to realize once you've been in Sobolton for a while is that a lot of things are waiting just beneath the surface. People who drive through the town, or who just stop for a little while, think that we live in a nice normal little place. I get that, I really do, but once you've been here for a while you start to see that there's a lot more going on. I'm sure people say that in a lot of towns, but here in Sobolton it's really true."

"I almost feel like you're trying to warn me about something," John admitted.

"I'm telling you to trust your instincts," she continued. "I was at that town hall meeting you called a while back, the one where you were talking about Little Miss Dead. I noticed how Joe Hicks acted, and I think you noticed too. That man is bad news, Mr. Tench. Worse than that, he's a menace to this town and to everyone good who lives here. You seem like someone who likes to treat people fairly, so I can imagine that you might hold back from forming too strong a judgment, but I want you to know that Joe Hicks can't be trusted."

"I admit that he's made some contradictory comments," John replied, "but I'm a little surprised to hear you talk about him this way."

"I've seen what he gets up to," she explained. "With my own eyes, and also through Tommy's comments as well. When I heard that Joe was being forced out, I felt hopeful for the first time in many years. I felt as if maybe, just maybe, this town might be able to breathe again. I can't prove it, John, but I have a strong suspicion that Joe Hicks has had his fingers in a lot of pies. That's one of the reasons I wanted Tommy to invite you tonight. I wanted to get a handle on you, to see whether you're like Joe or whether you're something better. And I see now that you're better. So much better."

"I do my best," John told her. "I wouldn't have moved up here otherwise."

"Don't trust Hicks," she said firmly. "I'm not telling you what to do, I'm just hoping that you'll listen to your own gut feeling on this matter. If Joe Hicks tells you that the sky's blue, look up to check." She saw that Tommy had looked over, and she took a moment to smile at him and wave. "Okay, John, how about dessert? You can handle that, can't you?"

"Absolutely," he replied as she walked away, although he couldn't help but wonder why she'd been so determined to warn him about his predecessor. "Thank you."

CHAPTER FOUR

Twenty years earlier...

"LET'S GET HIM IN here," Lisa said as she helped set the panting dog down onto her examination table. "I'm going to need to take out whatever's obstructing his airway."

"I don't know what happened," Liam Fowler said frantically, stopping in the doorway. "One moment we were out there in the forest and he was running around like usual, and then suddenly he could barely breathe!"

"Rachel, can you take Mr. Fowler through to the waiting room please?" Lisa said, "and then bring through everything I'm going to need to open little Rex up." She looked down at the terrier dog as it lay gasping and spluttering in front of her. "He's clearly swallowed something he shouldn't have."

"I thought he was going to die on the way over here," Liam said as Rachel led him away. "I drove like a maniac."

"Okay, Rex," Lisa said, placing two fingers against the underside of the dog's throat as she tried to work out exactly where to make her first incision. "I'm going to help you, but it might be a little uncomfortable first. Let's just work together and you're going to be back to normal in no time."

***

"Did you get it?" Liam asked around half an hour later, immediately getting to his feet as Lisa stepped out into the reception area. "Is he okay?"

"He's fine," she replied, clearly a little shaken after the emergency operation. "He's resting now, my assistant's putting in some stitches but there's no reason to think he won't make a full recovery."

"Did you find whatever was stuck in his throat?"

"I did," she said, heading to the counter and setting down a small plastic bag, then opening it and tipping out the contents. "Where exactly in the forest did you say you were when he got sick?"

"Not too far at all," Liam replied, making his way over and looking down at the objects on the counter. "Is that..."

"A ring," she said, turning the gold ring over so that he could see it better. "No wonder the poor little guy could barely breathe, this thing was almost completely blocking his pipes." She paused, before sliding a smaller, slightly gray object closer. "And I found this, too."

"What is it?" Liam asked. "Is it some kind of stone?"

"It was actually wedged inside the ring when I pulled it out," she explained. "It came loose during the operation, but originally the ring was around it." She took the ring and slid it back onto the gray object, until it was held fast. "I can't be completely certain, but my best bet is that this is part of a human finger."

"A human..."

Liam's voice trailed off as he stared down at the sight on the counter.

"Wait a moment," he continued, "are you seriously trying to tell me that my little Rex... ate a person's finger?"

"No, I'm saying that he *tried* to eat a person's finger," she replied, "and it got lodged in his throat."

"But where did it come from?"

"My guess? A hand."

"I get that, but why was it out in the forest?" He stared at the finger for a moment longer, before stepping back and partially turning away. "I'm sorry, I don't want to look at it. I'm feeling a little nauseous."

"It's old," Lisa replied. "Don't worry, I don't think this is fresh at all. There's absolutely no meat on it, and it looks pretty weather-worn. I wouldn't be surprised if it's been out there for a while." She pulled the piece of bone back out and held up the ring, turning it around so that she could see it from all sides. "This thing looks pretty valuable. It might even be real gold."

"You think someone would have missed it?" Liam asked, struggling to keep from throwing up.

"Well, and the finger too, obviously," Lisa pointed out. "Where in the forest did you say you were walking Rex, again?"

***

"Henge Cliff," she said, setting the ring and the bone down – separately – onto the desk in Joe's office. "Do you realize what this means?"

"Is that a finger?" Joe replied, leaning forward and peering at the piece of bone. "From a person?"

"Liam Fowler was walking his dog less than a mile away from Henge Cliff," Lisa continued, "and the dog came back with this thing wedged in its throat. Do you realize what this means?"

"That Liam Fowler had better have some good pet insurance?"

"It means the dog found parts of a human body," Lisa said, preferring to ignore Joe's attempts at humor. "I don't need to tell you why that might be extremely significant, given the location."

"Let's rewind a little," Joe replied cautiously. "Okay, I think this could be an important development. Obviously people don't go around losing fingers all the time, and I certainly know why Henge Cliff might be significant." He picked up the ring. "If this is one of the missing bodies from the bus, then I'd imagine we should be able to find someone in the town who can identify this ring." He tried to look at the inside of the band. "I don't see any kind of writing or -"

"It's not engraved," Lisa told him. "I already checked."

"Well, aren't you the little detective?" he chuckled, before wincing and sighing as he slowly hauled himself up from his chair. "You did the right thing bringing this to me, Lisa."

She waited, convinced that he was going to leap into action, but as the seconds passed she began to realize that he had no such intent. Sure enough, after a few seconds he set the bone down next to the ring and made his way out from behind the desk.

"Probably best not to mention this to too

many people," he continued, patting her on the shoulder, "at least not until I've been out there to take a look, which might take a day or two. We've got a lot on our plates here at the station right now, what with one thing and another, so cold cases aren't exactly a priority. But I *will* get out there just as soon as I can, and I'll be sure to let you know if I find anything. Don't get your hopes up, though, because that stretch of forest was already checked pretty thoroughly back in the day."

"I thought you'd send a team out there right away," she told him.

"What team? Have you seen my budget report for the rest of the financial year?" He started steering her out of the office and into the corridor. "There are a whole lot of zeroes in there, and most of them aren't in the right place. Gotta move 'em on over from the right side of the columns to the left. Or is it from the left to the right? I don't know, I've never been good with that sort of thing, but the gist is I can't go sending so-called 'teams' out to do anything right now."

"People will want to know if another body has been found."

"Which is why we have to take this slowly, and not arouse false hope," he explained as they passed the reception desk and headed to the station's front door. "False hope's the worst thing in the world, and you have to remember that there are people alive in this town for whom this remains a very... immediate issue. Three men are still missing all these years later and we want to respect their memories rather than turning this into some kind of circus."

"But -"

"But you're a smart girl and I'm sure you know all that," he added, interrupting her again as he opened the door and eased her out, before stopping to smile at her. "Remember what I said, just keep this to yourself right now and everything'll be just fine. I promise." He paused, watching her carefully as if he was studying every facet of her reaction, as if he was checking to make sure she'd bought what he was selling. "You trust me, Lisa, don't you?"

"Of course," she lied.

"Then that's sorted," he replied. "I'll keep you informed if and when I make any progress, but don't expect it too soon." He began to ease the door shut. "Good luck back at work. I'm sure there are lots of cats and dogs and hamsters and whatnot that'll be needing your help."

Left standing alone on the steps at the front of the station, Lisa couldn't help but feel that – even by his usual standards – Joe had been remarkably evasive. She was fully used to him being dismissive, sometimes even downright rude, but he'd clearly been keen to avoid getting into too much detail about the bone she'd found, and she couldn't help but worry that he was going to try to sweep the whole thing under the carpet. None of that made sense, of course, because she figured that anyone who helped find one of the missing bodies would be treated as a hero, in which case he should be all over the situation, but...

But instead he'd seemed almost annoyed by the development. And as she turned and made her way down the icy steps, taking care not to slip, Lisa couldn't help but wonder why Joe Hicks was acting so strangely.

CHAPTER FIVE

Today...

"NO, THANK YOU AGAIN," John said as he and Tommy made their way along the corridor, heading toward his office. "I enjoyed dinner last night a great deal. I'd offer to reciprocate, but my cooking and hosting skills really aren't up to scratch."

"Oh, that's fine," Tommy said a little hurriedly, almost as if he was panicking at the thought of another dinner party. "Tracy and I really just wanted to welcome you to the town, that's all."

"Which you did magnificently," John replied, stepping into his office. "You have a lovely little family, Tommy, and -"

Before he could finish, he saw an elderly woman sitting in a chair in front of his desk. He opened his mouth to ask who she was, but then he turned to see Doctor Robert Law slowly and slightly painfully easing himself up from the sofa in the far corner.

"Carolyn wasn't at the desk," Robert said, "so we took the liberty of showing ourselves in. I'm sorry about that, John, but this is a delicate matter and we need your help."

"I'll... go and make some coffee," Tommy stammered, turning and hurrying out of the room.

"I came to you directly," Robert continued, leaning on his cane as he made his way over, "because I didn't want to leave much of a paper-trail. The truth is, Susan and I would both like to keep this situation rather under the radar, since it's so delicate. Plus, that approach seems only fitting, since your predecessor took very much the same approach."

***

"I remember it like it was yesterday," Susan said, with tears in her eyes as she sat staring down at the paperwork on John's desk. "The last forty years seem to fade to nothing, and it's like I'm there again on my wedding day. On *our* wedding day. It was supposed to be the happiest, gayest day in the town's history."

"You must forgive me," John replied

cautiously, glancing briefly at Robert again before turning back to Susan. "I'm still getting to know the history of the town."

"Ten weddings," she continued, "all on the same day. It was a coincidence at first, but then someone or other thought it might be fun to combine the weddings into one big event. At first I wasn't sure about it, I'd been planning my wedding day since I was a young girl and I just wanted a nice quiet event where I could show my love for my darling Timothy. I wanted a summer wedding, but the organizers got it into their heads that we should use the event to mark some big winter moment. So I was persuaded that we should join in, and the day itself began so wonderfully. There are lots of photos of the ten brides and the ten grooms."

"It was all set up to be one big party," Robert added.

"So the weddings happened," Susan explained, "out at the waterfall a few miles from town. We were all going to be driven by bus back into town, and someone – I forget who – had the idea that the brides should go on one bus and the grooms should go on another. We all got onboard, but there was a problem with the grooms' bus. We were assured it wouldn't be an issue, so the bus with the brides went ahead, and all the guests accompanied them, and the grooms were supposed to follow. One of them, Pat Mayfair, was the driver and he was also an accomplished mechanic. So the rest of us arrived in town and prepared for the party, and we waited for our new husbands to arrive."

She fell silent, and by this point John was already starting to guess what must have happened next.

"Hours passed," she told him, sniffing back more tears, "and then more hours, and soon it was starting to get dark. We tried not to worry, we told ourselves that Pat was simply having trouble getting the motor started. Eventually someone went to check, but he came back later and said he couldn't find them. It was as if they'd just vanished into thin air somewhere between here and the waterfall. That's when search parties went out, although I remember most of us thought it was all just part of some foolish prank. We believed that our new husbands were playing a joke, and that soon they'd leap out from hiding and start laughing at us. But then as night fell, that prospect seemed less and less likely. Then someone noticed the damage on the side of the road."

"This was before the guardrails," Robert said ominously.

"There were tire marks leading off the precipice," Susan continued. "In the darkness, it was so hard for anyone to work out what had really happened. By the time the sun came up, we'd pieced together the fact that the bus must have crashed. In the morning it was found mangled at the bottom of a steep cliff out at Henge Cliff. It had fallen at least thirty meters, and probably rolled as well. There were seven bodies in the bus, and..."

She paused, before turning to Robert.

"You were involved," she reminded him. "Did they really die on impact, or was that just something that was said to make us feel better?"

"They almost certainly died on impact," he replied. "They were the lucky ones."

"Three were still missing," Susan told John. "There was some evidence to suggest that they'd crawled out of the wreckage, or... that they'd been dragged out. There were lots of conflicting rumors swirling, but they were certainly gone from the site of the crash. My Timothy was one of them and -"

Before she could finish, she burst into tears. John immediately slid a box of tissues across the desk, and Robert took one and handed it to Susan. Both men waited as she dabbed at her eyes, but she was clearly incapable of saying anything more, at least for now.

"The search went on for weeks," Robert explained, picking up the story. "A few scraps were found, some hints, but nothing definitive. The most popular theory at the time was that the three survivors made their way out of the wreckage and headed away from the site, trying to get back up to the road somehow. And then, whatever happened next, they ended up not making it."

"Were they ever found?" John asked.

Robert shook his head.

"They're still out there somewhere," Susan whimpered, as she took another tissue from the box. "They've been out there for forty years, unable to settle, unable to rest because no-one has found their bodies and treated them with the respect they -"

She burst into tears again, unable to continue.

"Every so often," Robert said after a moment, "people go out and take another look, but they never really find much. The sheriff's department has assisted on a few occasions, but to be honest with you, John... your predecessor Mr. Hicks never showed much interest in reviving the investigation. He paid lip service to it, of course, but most of us got the sense that he wasn't truly interested in getting to the bottom of whatever had happened. He always said he was too busy, or he didn't have the resources, or that the weather was about to turn... he always had an excuse ready. But now Susan's the only widow left from the ten women who married that day, and she's worried that no-one else is going to care."

"I've always been so sure that my Timothy would be found eventually," Susan sobbed. "Now, for the first time, I'm scared that he won't."

"I brought her here today because I was

hoping you might be able to help," Robert continued. "John, after forty years the chances of finding anything are slim to none, but one final official search might throw up some scrap of evidence, just enough to let the town start to move on. At the last memorial service for the tragedy, only four people turned up, including Susan and myself."

"One day there might be none," Susan cried. "The next ceremony's coming up and I can't bear to think of how little interest there'll be. No-one will care, and eventually it'll all be forgotten. I just can't think of poor Timothy and the others never finding their way home to a proper resting place."

"Is there anything you can do, John?" Robert asked. "Can we organize one final push to see if the truth might still be out there after all these years?"

"We're overstretched as it is," John told him, before looking at Susan as she continued to cry. He knew he didn't have a spare cent in the budget, or a spare minute in his day, but at the same time he also knew that he couldn't simply stand back and do nothing at all. "But we'll figure out a way," he added finally. "If we can find those men, we will. And we'll bring them home."

AMY CROSS

CHAPTER SIX

Twenty years earlier...

SNOW WAS FALLING STEADILY from the sky, as it had fallen steadily for weeks now, drifting down past the edge of the road and past the parked police cruiser, past the rocky wall and down to the narrow space at the bottom at the side of the forest.

Wincing and struggling with each step, Sheriff Joe Hicks finally reached the foot of the narrow, steep path that led down from the road. He was out of breath and out of sorts, huffing and puffing as he reached out to steady himself; he had to stop and take a moment to pull himself together, and already he was starting to wonder whether he'd made the right decision, whether he'd really *had* to venture out alone. Glancing over his shoulder, he saw the narrow path and realized that climbing back up would be twice as hard, but he told himself that he'd deal with that problem when it arose. For now...

For now, he had another problem on his mind.

Reaching into his pocket, he took out a handkerchief; opening the edges, he saw the scrap of bone and the gold ring, and he let out a heavy sigh as he pondered once more whether or not he was doing the right thing.

At that moment, as if to offer some kind of perverse answer, a gust of wind ripped and howled through the forest, almost screaming into the white sky.

"Yeah yeah," Joe muttered, weighing the bone and ring in his hand for a moment longer before stepping out across the snowy ground, approaching the trees. "I get it."

Reaching the edge of the forest, he looked between the trees and saw nothing but darkness and gloom spread off into the distance. He hesitated for a few seconds, watching in case there might be even the slightest hint of movement or the faintest snapping of a twig, but he felt a rush of relief as he realized that the forest seemed utterly empty and utterly uninterested in his presence. That, more than anything, was what he'd been hoping for.

"Alright," he said finally, "so there was a...

leak of some sort, but it was an accident and now I'm returning it."

He began to crouch down, wincing as he felt a sharp pain in his knees. After setting the handkerchief down, he used his hands to dig a small hole in the hard ground, and then he tucked the bone and the ring down deep before covering them again with dirt and snow.

"There," he continued, "it's done. See?"

He looked up, but the only witnesses were the tall bare trees that rose up high all around. Still, as the wind howled again, Joe knew that those trees might well be witnesses enough, and that they might whisper the news deeper into the forest.

"So no trouble," he sneered as he stood up again. "It's no-one's fault that this happened, it was just some damn dog that dug 'em up. And if you ask me, that's not on us, that's on you. You have to keep your own secrets sometimes, you can't rely on others doing it for you all the time. So... do better, okay?"

He waited, although he wasn't really sure what for, and then he turned and began to make his way back to the narrow path. Sure enough, climbing back up to the side of the road was much harder than the journey down, and he really had to put his back into the effort; he felt a twinge or two in his spine, and he was out of breath before he'd made it ten feet, but he figured that he'd just have to take regular breaks along the way. Which is exactly what he did as he clambered back up toward the road, keen to get back into town and forget that Lisa Sondnes had ever turned up in his office with those strange items at all.

Job done.

***

"Okay, but I really don't see what any of this has to do with my department," Joe complained with a heavy sigh as Carolyn followed him through to his office. "You're new here so I understand that you're not sure how these things work, but let me be clear about one thing."

Reaching the desk, he stopped and turned to her so suddenly that she almost slammed straight into him.

"I'm here to solve crimes," he said firmly. "Actual crimes. So when somebody comes along complaining about a fence that's too high, or a cat that meows too loudly at night, I don't care." He took some of the papers from her hands. "I don't want to know a damn thing about all these silly, trifling little disputes that happen around the town. I've more than got my hands full with actual cases. Is that clear?"

"Absolutely, Sheriff Hicks," Carolyn replied. "I'm sorry, you're right, I'm just having a little trouble... getting up to speed."

"You'll learn," he said, handing the papers back to her. "Now get back to work."

As she hurried out of the room, he watched her backside for a moment before turning to go over to his desk. And then, stopping mid-stride, he was shocked to see the gold ring and the fragment of bone resting next to his box of pens.

"Carolyn?" he called out.

"Yes?"

She scurried back in, clearly worried that she'd done something wrong.

"What are *those* doing there?" he asked, pointing at the offending objects.

"What do you mean?" she asked, stepping over to the desk and looking down. "Do you mean the pens of -"

"I mean those things," he continued, his voice positively dripping with disdain. "How did they get back here? Who brought them in?"

"Well, I don't know," she replied. "I don't think I've ever seen them before."

"I'm not having silly games played in my office," he said firmly. "Carolyn, if someone came in here, they'd have had to have walked right past your desk so you must have seen them!"

"I didn't see anyone!" she protested, before peering more closely at the items. "What is that, anyway? Is it part of a bone?"

"I'm sick and tried of this foolishness," Joe muttered, taking a handkerchief from his pocket and scooping the bone and ring up, then turning to her. "Woman, I need you to think. Someone has to have walked in here and put these on my desk, and it can't have happened long ago because..." He paused as he tried to make sense of the timeline. "Because they'd have had to have made it back into town before me, which I don't quite get because I didn't stop anywhere along the way. I just drove back straight along the road, I parked outside and I came in here. I talked to you for a moment at the desk, but that's the only time when I would've given anyone a chance to get ahead of me."

"Ahead of you?"

"Who the hell did this?" he hissed, storming to the door and looking both ways along the corridor, clearly on the verge of boiling over with rage. "I'm not a figure of fun! I won't be ridiculed like this, especially not at my own place of work!"

He turned to her.

"If you know who did this," he continued, "then now's the time to be honest, because if I find out later that you're in cahoots with anyone, you'll be out of this job so fast you won't even know what hit you!"

"I don't know anything, I swear," she replied, before looking at the handkerchief he was still holding in his right hand. "What... I hope you don't mind me asking you this, but... what are those things? It looks like a ring and... some kind of piece of bone."

She waited, but Joe was glaring at her as if he was still trying to decide whether or not she was telling the truth. After a moment he narrowed his gaze a little, squinting to get a better view, yet somehow he seemed to have still not made up his mind whether to trust her. The longer this silence persisted, the more Carolyn felt uncomfortable until finally she worried that she simply had to say something – anything – to settle the atmosphere.

"No-one came past the desk, Sir," she said plaintively. "Not recently, at least. In fact, it's been quite a quiet morning. I was just thinking that earlier, about how there haven't been many people here. It's just been a very calm and relaxing morning with only a few fairly unimportant calls."

"Then there's only one person it can be," Joe sneered, clenching both fists as he felt the anger bubbling away inside his belly. "I'm an idiot. I should have figured this out right from the start."

CHAPTER SEVEN

Today...

"WHY?" GREG SAID AS he flicked a switch on the wall, bringing the lights high above to life. "Well, to be honest with you, no-one ever told me to get rid of it. That's why."

Stepping through into the storage area at the rear of the garage, John felt a shiver run through his bones as soon as he spotted the twisted, mangled wreckage that had clearly once been a bus. Much of the frame had been burned many years earlier, and the top section – particularly around the front – was heavily mangled. As he stopped and stared at the bus, with his breath visible in the cold air, John couldn't help but feel that no-one could ever have survived such an accident.

"There's a lot of stuff that's been kicking around for years," Greg continued. "It's evidence, so I can't exactly decide to get rid of it myself. Besides, as you can see, I've got plenty of room."

"Susan, wait!" Robert called out from the corridor. "I don't think this is a good idea!"

Behind John, Susan Walpole stepped into the hangar, with Robert Law leaning on his cane and limping along just a few steps further back. As soon as she spotted the mangled bus, however, Susan stopped just a couple of paces behind John, transfixed by the awful sight. For a few seconds she seemed almost transported to another world, or perhaps more pertinently to another time.

"I knew it was here," she whispered, "all these years, but somehow I could never bring myself to come and see it until now."

"Let's go back over to the station," Robert said cautiously. "Susan, I think this is going to be far too upsetting for you."

"On the contrary," she replied, taking a step forward, "I think perhaps I've waited far too long for this moment."

"So this is the bus that crashed forty years ago?" John said, tilting his head a little as he looked at the wreckage. "All perfectly preserved in here after all this time."

"I'll be back in the shop," Greg said, turning and heading through the door. "You know, if you need me. Which you won't."

"There was plenty of talk of getting rid of it," Robert explained. "Joe Hicks certainly wanted it gone, but there was some bureaucratic or procedural reason why he couldn't. Something about the paperwork .The way I understand it, to get rid of the evidence, he'd have had to have re-designated the case as closed, and even when he took office many years after the crash he didn't feel he could make that move. He was kind of stuck in a bind, so his solution was to store the thing away like this and... forget about it, I guess."

"I assume it was analyzed properly," John said, stepping over to the bus but stopping short of actually touching what remained of its metal frame. "There was a full forensic analysis?"

"Sure," Robert replied, "but that was back in 1984, when there wouldn't have been such advanced tools. And by the time those tools *were* available, Joe Hicks refused to do anything."

John turned to him.

"Money matters," Robert added, clearly unconvinced. "Joe's answer whenever anyone asked him to do something he didn't much fancy."

"We certainly have a budget to keep to," John said, turning to look at the bus again, before reaching out to touch the mangled metal. "But -"

"Don't!" Susan said firmly.

John turned to look at her.

"Just to be safe," she continued, making her way over to join him. "It sings sometimes. Mostly at night, but I often think that's simply when it's easier to hear. The air's thinner and the sound travels further." She reached out with a black-gloved hand and touched the bus herself. "Once you've heard it," she added, "you can't entirely stop, and I'm not sure you want to open that particular door, Mr. Tench. I did once, years ago, and I've never quite recovered. The new barrier out at the crash site is much the same, it sings the same song. It's the song that the dead sing."

John opened his mouth to reply, before glancing back at Robert, who in turn nodded sagely. Unable to quite work out how best to interpret that gesture, John looked at Susan again and saw that she seemed lost in thought as she continued to touch the bus.

"I hear them so clearly these days," she added, as a single tear ran down her cheek. "I think they know I'm the last of the widows. I think they know I'm their last chance for justice."

"Justice?" John replied.

"There was no good reason for the crash," Susan said firmly, "and I realized immediately that there was a cover-up. That conviction has only strengthened over the years. The truth about those ten deaths has never come out, Mr Tench, but it will. It must." She turned to him, her eyes filled with a kind of steely determination. "I refuse to accept any other outcome."

***

"She's a feisty woman," Robert said as he and John stood on the steps at the front of the station, watching Susan walking away through the snow. "Don't think for one second that she'll simply give up and forget, because she won't. She's always been on this crusade, and she won't rest until she's got answers."

"Do you really think there's any way to uncover the truth?" John asked. "Even assuming, that is, that there are answers to uncover. Why couldn't the crash have been an accident? I've seen some of the roads round these parts. Even in good weather, I'm sure some of them are treacherous."

"True," Robert said with a faint smile, but after a few seconds the smile faded. "The thing is, John, I've got skin in this game. I courted Susan Walpole when I was young, back when she was regular Susan Sanders. I even asked her father for permission to marry her."

"And?"

"The old bastard turned me down."

"Why?"

"Because he thought I'd never finish medical school," Robert continued, "and to be fair, at the time he had a point. I was quite an undisciplined kid. A rebel, you might say."

"I find that hard to believe," John said with a grin.

"The point is, if he'd agreed, we might very well have delayed our wedding until the big day when everyone else was getting married." Robert hesitated for a few seconds. "I'm sure you understand the implication."

"You could very easily have been one of the men on that bus."

Robert nodded.

"I'll see what I can do," John said, as he saw Susan disappearing around a corner in the distance, "although our resources are somewhat limited at the moment. I can certainly review the evidence, cast a fresh eye over things, that sort of thing. You never know, being an outsider, I might spot something that went unnoticed before."

"There's one thing you won't find in any of the files," Robert replied. "A little birdie once told me that a finger showed up about twenty years ago, along with a ring that had belonged to one of the dead men. It was Timothy Walpole's ring, actually."

"Was it ever handed in?"

"It was, but you won't find any mention in the files."

"Why not?"

"Because the esteemed Joe Hicks liked to

68

handle things his own way," Robert explained. "Handy for him, but not so handy for anyone who'd like to follow the rules and build on the work of those who went before him." He checked his watch. "I have an appointment soon, so I need to get going, but can you please just look into the case a little? As you said, an outsider's point of view might just be crucial, and I really want to try to put Susan's mind at rest. She's... a dear friend, and I hate to see her suffering like this."

"I'll do my best," John replied.

"That's all any of us can promise," Robert said, picking his way carefully down the steps and adjusting his cap, before stopping to look back up at John. "Oh, and by the way, I received some interesting news by email this morning. Do you remember the berries I said were in Little Miss Dead's stomach when she died? Well, it turns out that they're more unusual than I thought, and they're pretty much only found in this part of the country. Wherever she'd been before she died, it can't have been more than a few hundred miles away. Or it seems very unlikely, at least."

"I don't suppose you've got any more revelations for me, have you?"

"I'm working as fast as I can," Robert insisted as he began to walk away, briefly lifting his cap as a mark of respect. "I never promised miracles, John. I'm more your hard-working, nose-to-the-grindstone kind of guy."

CHAPTER EIGHT

Twenty years earlier...

"WHAT THE HELL?"

Kneeling on the floor in her kitchen, Lisa peered at the small white flakes on the counter-top. She'd been finding the exact same things for a few weeks now, dotted around the apartment here and there, and she'd even noticed a few at the office; she used a fingertip to move the flakes around, and she couldn't shake the feeling that they seemed to be particles of skin. She looked up at the ceiling and noticed nothing untoward, and then – getting to her feet – she leaned over the counter and ran a hand repeatedly through her hair.

Nothing fell out.

"Have I got a ghost?" she muttered, still

puzzled by the flakes. "A ghost with dandruff?"

Before she had a chance to ponder the puzzle further, she heard a knock at the door. Making her way over, she pulled the door open and was surprised to find Sheriff Joe Hicks standing outside.

"Hey," she said, "what -"

"What do you think you're doing?" he snapped angrily.

"I beg your -"

"Do you think you're funny?" he continued. "Do you think you're some kind of comedian, Lisa?"

"I don't know what you -"

"How did you even do it, huh?" he asked. "How did you make it back to town before me? And how did you know I'd be out there?"

"Joe, I have no idea what you're talking about," she said firmly. "Do you want to come inside and explain? I'm happy to help, but I can only do that if I at least have a clue what's going on."

"I'm not coming inside and sitting down with you," he said, raising a hand and pointing directly into her face, "but let me make one thing very clear. You've been causing me trouble lately, Lisa. First with your report about a supposed wolf, then with all that nonsense about Wentworth Stone, and now by trying to dig up this whole mess out at Henge Cliff. You might find this sort of thing amusing, Lisa, but I want to remind you that you're treading on very thin ground. I won't tolerate this type of behavior."

"Joe -"

"I'm going to take it back out there one more time," he added, cutting her off yet again, "and that's going to be the end of the matter. And if you pull another stunt, then I will bring so many bad things raining down on top of you, you won't even remember your own name. Don't forget, either, that I can pull strings. I had a lot of respect for your father, Lisa, but that only gets you so far. There are certain agreements that can and will be revisited if you try pulling more stunts."

"Agreements?" she replied. "Stunts? Joe, you're not making any sense at all."

"I'm making all the sense I need to make," he replied, sounding a little out of breath now as he turned and began to walk away. "Don't act dumb with me, Lisa. If you try, you'll learn very fast that you're severely out of your depth. And don't tell anyone about this conversation. It's private, it's between me and you! I thought you'd be smart enough to realize that by now!"

"I still don't know what you're talking about," she insisted, but he was already heading back to his car and she quickly realized that there was no point following. At the same time, his outburst made no sense whatsoever. "What am I supposed to have done?"

***

"There!" Joe hissed a short while later, as he once again pushed the bone and ring into the ground, before covering them with a little more dirt and snow than before. "And this time, you'd better *stay* buried!"

Wincing as he got to his feet, he looked around. He was back in the same spot as earlier, at the foot of the cliff beyond the side of the road; he looked out into the trees and saw nothing but gloom, and with the sun starting to set he felt the air chill a little as snow continued to drift down. He'd been annoyed at having to venture out to Henge Cliff once already, so making the journey twice in one day was utterly infuriating, and he couldn't help but worry that Lisa might still be trying to make him look like a fool.

"Do you hear me, Lisa?" he called out, just in case she might be hiding somewhere. "I'm not the kind of man who makes empty threats."

He waited, but there was no sign of her at all.

"Yeah, that's right," he muttered, turning and starting to make his way up the path once more, heading back toward his cruiser parked by the side of the road. "When Joe Hicks talks, people listen, and if they don't then they soon learn the seriousness of their mistake. I'm respected round these parts and there's a reason for that."

For the next few minutes he struggled slightly to get all the way up the hill, but finally he reached the cruiser and stopped for a moment to get his breath back. He still saw no sign of anyone nearby, and he knew that there was no other easy way up to the road; anyone else down there, if they wanted to avoid being seen, would have to go miles out of their way, and he felt confident that there wasn't a person alive who could make that journey back to Sobolton faster than he was going to manage. Evidently Lisa had slipped past him earlier, but he told himself that this time he was paying attention.

Unlocking the cruiser's door, he climbed inside out of the snow and let out a heavy grunt as he leaned back in his seat. He slammed the door shut and slid his keys into the ignition, and then he froze as he spotted two small objects resting on the passenger seat next to him.

The finger.

And the ring.

"What..."

Looking around, he saw nothing but the bare, desolate snow-covered road. His first thought was that somehow Lisa must have managed to clamber up to the cruiser again, even though he knew that this was impossible; after a few seconds, however, he remembered that he'd locked the cruiser before going down to the bottom of the cliff, and a shiver passed through his bones as he realized that for all her smarts, Lisa wasn't some kind of genius.

Which meant...

"No," he whispered, picking up the bone and the ring, just to check that they were real. "Why now? Come on, this isn't fair."

He waited, desperately trying to come up with some other explanation, even though deep down he knew that there was really only one possibility.

"This is *not* fair," he said again, through clenched teeth, but he knew that this time he couldn't ignore the message. He stared at the offending objects for a moment longer, before squeezing them tight in his fist and then climbing back out of the cruiser. "Why do I always have to clean up messes left behind by other people, huh? Why do I even have to be involved in this at all?"

Slamming the cruiser's door shut much, much harder than before – in an attempt to make his anger perfectly clear – he picked his way carefully across the snow and ice until he reached the metal guardrail at the side of the road. Placing his hands on the top of the guardrail, he leaned over and looked back down at the edge of the forest far below. He waited, but after a few seconds he began to notice a faint vibration running through the guardrail and entering his hands, almost like...

Almost like music.

"Stop that!" he hissed, pulling his hands away. "I'm not weak-minded, okay? I'm no kind of -"

And then, before he could finish, he spotted a figure far below, standing in the snow and staring back up at him. He squinted, but against the brightness of the snow this figure merely looked dark; at the same time, Joe recognized its silhouette and he knew exactly who had come to greet him. He swallowed hard, wondering whether there was any chance he could just drive away and pretend that the whole situation hadn't happened, but he knew that wouldn't work and – besides – he could feel the figure's eyes burning into him as if daring him to even try to run. He'd already been called back once, and he knew that he didn't dare make the same mistake twice.

"Alright," he whispered, despite the fear in his chest. "Fine. Have it your way. But whatever you've got to say, you should have said it last time. You can't just snap your fingers and expect me to keep running out here like this."

AMY CROSS

CHAPTER NINE

Today...

TWISTED METAL CREAKED AND groaned beneath his feet as John gripped the old railing and climbed up into what was left of the bus. He had to duck down to avoid hitting his head on part of the roof that had been crushed down toward the driver's compartment, and he couldn't help but note that overall there was now very little space for a man to move around inside the wreckage.

Stopping, he looked at the rows of contorted seats, each of which had been crushed slightly differently. In some cases the roof had been ripped down, leaving glinting metal edges hanging down in the low light; in other parts of the bus the seats looked relatively intact, although as he made a quick count of the number of places, John realized that the bus would easily have held a couple of dozen passengers. Survival, then, would have been based on where a person was sitting, and if the passengers had all been grouped in the space near the front then it wasn't hard to see how they would have died.

Picking his way carefully past the first couple of twisted, gnarly seats, John saw dark stains on the fabric of some of the seats. He stopped and reached into his pocket, taking out some old photos that he'd pulled from the files; sure enough, he saw figures slumped in those same seats, their bodies wrecked by the force of the impact and in some cases cut apart by the broken metal. One of the men had been found still sitting upright save for a deep slice on one side of the neck; his head was hanging to the left at an unnatural angle, as if it had been partially torn away and then left to dangle. At the bottom of the image, a date had been stamped in white lettering.

1984.

Sometimes, John mused, 1984 didn't feel like history. He remembered that year, albeit as a child. Now, suddenly, 1984 was four decades ago, when he'd grown up thinking that 'four decades ago' meant the Second World War or -

Suddenly he heard something bump against the outside of the bus. He climbed over a couple of seats and looked out through the broken window, but he saw no sign of anyone else in the garage. He waited, telling himself that there was no need to be jumpy, and then he pulled back inside the wrecked bus and looked around again. A moment later, glancing at one of the railings, he peered more closely and spotted what appeared to be a set of thick grooves cut through the metal.

Like claws.

"Let's not get ahead of ourselves," he muttered, and as those words left his lips he saw his own breath in the cold air.

For a moment he merely stood and contemplated the silence of the wreckage. The crash would have been chaotic and violent, with glass shattering and metal being crushed as the bus tumbled down off the side of the road; the impact at the bottom would have been even greater, and even when the bus finally came to a halt there would have been the dying gasps of anyone unlucky enough to have survived the first phase of the accident. As John turned and looked toward the rear of the bus, he once again contemplated the fate of the three men whose bodies had never been found, who might just have been able to crawl out of the wreckage and -

Suddenly something hit the bus again, causing the vehicle to shudder briefly with such force that John almost lost his footing.

"Who's there?" he called out, hurrying to another window and looking out as the bus fell still again. "Is someone out there? Show yourself!"

He waited, but already deep down he knew he was unlikely to get an answer. After looking around one more time, he began to make his way carefully out of the wrecked bus, before clambering through the door and stepping out into the garage. He stopped and looked at the photos again, and he found himself particularly interested in one that showed the bus as it had been found at the foot of the cliff, resting on its side with so much broken glass and metal scattered all around. From experience with road traffic accidents, John knew that the scene would have been bad, with lots of blood and dismembered body parts.

And then, as he began to look at a wider shot of the accident site, he heard footsteps racing past. Surprised, he turned just as the footsteps seemed to run behind the wrecked bus, and a moment later silence returned.

"Hello?" he said, concerned that somehow a local child had managed to break into the garage. "Who are you?"

Reaching the other side, he saw no-one, but a moment later someone started laughing; again, the intruder had made their way to the opposite end of the bus, and John once more hurried around only to find himself staring at empty space.

The laughter, meanwhile, had drifted away but could still just about be heard.

"Who is it?" John asked, although he was already thinking back to the sight of Little Miss Dead – a nickname he hated – standing in his office. "I'm not interested in games. If there's someone here and you have something to say to me, you might as well come out with it."

He waited again, and after a few seconds he heard calmer, slower footsteps approaching. Turning, he saw the dead girl stepping out from behind the other end of the wrecked bus.

"You're not real," he said firmly.

The girl stared back at him with the same intensity that he remembered from the office, as if she expected him to react in a certain way. In the gloom of the garage, with precious little light breaking through the grimy high windows, John struggled to make out too many details of the girl at all, but he could see that she was wearing the same dress that he'd shown to the crowd in the town hall. And as she looked once more at her eyes, he felt a kind of yearning need reaching out to him and reminding him that he still hadn't made much progress in her case.

"I'm working on it," he stammered, feeling a sudden need to explain himself. "It's hard without a name. To be honest, I can't believe that three weeks into the case no-one has come forward to say they're missing you."

The girl offered no reply, preferring instead to simply stare back at him.

"I still don't think you're real," he continued, "but on the off-chance that you are, staring at me isn't going to help a great deal. So why don't you tell me something? Or if you're scared or shy, why don't you just give me some kind of clue? Right now, I'll take anything."

He watched the girl, but she seemed reluctant to even step out entirely from behind the bus. Whereas back in the office she'd seemed defiant and unafraid to be seen, now the opposite was true and she appeared to be holding back, lingering far enough back that she couldn't possibly be reached.

"Here's the thing," John said. "In any investigation, you start searching and you find clues real fast. Sometimes big clues and sometimes small clues, but at least there's something to go on. But with you, there's absolutely nothing. We've just got the autopsy report, which hasn't told us very much, and..."

He tried to think of some other scraps of information that might prove hopeful, but nothing came to mind and after a few seconds the girl began to shake her head sadly.

"What's that supposed to mean?" John asked, worried that in some way he'd failed her.

Still keeping her eyes fixed on him, the girl shook her head for a moment longer before turning and looking past him, watching the doorway.

John glanced over his shoulder, but he saw no sign that anyone else was about to join them.

"For a hallucination from my subconscious mind," he continued, turning to her again and seeing that she was still focused on the doorway, "you're not being much help. I thought you were supposed to be helping me untangle things in my head but -"

Suddenly the girl screamed, and a fraction of a second later she stepped back and vanished into thin air.

"Wait!" John called out, taking a step forward but then stopping as he realized that she was already gone. He waited for a moment, and then – hearing more footsteps – he turned just in time to see Joe Hicks appearing in the doorway.

"John," Joe said, sounding distinctly less cheery than usual, "Carolyn told me I'd find you in here. I've been hearing some interesting rumors about what you're up to. I think we need to talk in my... your office." He paused, as if he expected John to immediately rush over and obey. "Now."

CHAPTER TEN

Twenty years earlier...

STANDING AT THE FOOT of Henge Cliff, on the exact spot where the bus had crashed down all those years ago, Sheriff Joe Hicks stared into the forest and saw a dark figure watching him from between two trees.

"Well, I'm here," Joe said finally, unable to hide a sense of exasperation. "Are you happy now? I came out here. Twice, in fact."

He waited for a reply, even though he knew that most likely none would be forthcoming.

"I'm tired of this enigmatic shit," he muttered under his breath, before taking a moment to clear his throat. "Listen," he continued, raising his voice again so that he could be heard, "I'm a busy man. I've got a town to run. I thought we had it agreed that we wouldn't... waste each other's time like this."

The figure remained shrouded in darkness, its features impossible to make out, but Joe knew it was staring straight back at him.

"I should have known to expect something like this," he continued, "but would it really kill you to make contact like a normal person? You could call me back, or write to me. Failing that, you could send a telegram or... I don't know, get a message to me some other way. Normal people don't use bones and rings and all that stuff. And if you hadn't noticed by now, I'm a pretty straightforward kind of guy, and that's a quality I appreciate a great deal in other people. Could we not at least try to get on the same wavelength?"

Already feeling his frustration starting to grow, Joe looked down at the bone and the gold ring in the palm of his hand.

"I didn't want to see these," he added. "This is one of those situations that really doesn't need to get brought up again, don't you think? I mean, what exactly do you think is gonna come out of this? I wouldn't have though that anyone benefits from -"

Suddenly he froze, still staring between the trees as his eyes began to water.

"We didn't make this decision lightly," he continued, his voice trembling with tension now as the first tear escaped his left eye and began to run down his cheek. "We're not the ones who made the provocation. You're not supposed to interfere in our world, yet one of your number came crashing into our domain and caused so much harm and damage. And we recognized her."

Joe swallowed hard.

"I know who you're talking about," he said, still staring at the distant figure. "She didn't mean any harm. I've known her for a long time, she's a good person at heart, she was just trying to help and it all kinda spiraled out of control from there and -"

He let out a gasp.

"We recognized her," he added, as his voice became tighter and more guttural. "We agreed to let her live last time. We showed mercy and she came back to hurt us again."

Joe shook his head.

"No," he continued. "No, that's not quite right. As I understand it -"

He gasped again.

"One of us was in need of help," he said after a moment, as the other voice once more spoke through his mouth, "but it was not her business. She stole some cubs and they had to be retrieved. Their father went for them, but in the process he was injured. Now he's trapped between forms and there's nothing any of us can do to help him. The silver is like a poison, and it's driving him mad. He's not dead yet, but he will die from this eventually and we consider this to be an assassination."

He fell silent, and after a few seconds Joe felt himself regaining control over his own voice.

"Now, listen to me," he stammered, "I appreciate that there was an unfortunate situation and that it didn't get fixed as speedily as it might have, but -"

In that instant he felt a sharp pain in his throat. Dropping to his knees, he felt for a moment as if he couldn't breathe.

"There will have to be some form of redress," he gasped, as he felt another force pushing the words out through his own mouth. "The one who caused this damage must pay a price. That is how things have always worked. We were persuaded last time to show great mercy, and some of us at the time thought this was a mistake. Those voices grow louder now, and the rest of us are minded to agree. No-one should be allowed to harm us twice and get away with it. Where is the other man? Where is the one who stood with you last time?"

"Gone," Joe said as he took control of his voice again. "He was a good man, but he died."

"He might have been a good man," he added, as he began to taste blood at the back of his mouth, "but he encouraged all of us to make the wrong choice. Now you stand alone, and the time has come for the original decision to be reversed. She must pay for what she has done to us."

"You started this!" Joe hissed, struggling to keep from panicking. "You started it right here in this very spot!" He stamped a foot against the icy ground, in a desperate attempt to make his point. "Or if you didn't start it, you certainly escalated it! One of you attacked that bus, it came off the road and one of you... or more of you... you didn't hang around, did you? You took your chance to butcher the survivors. I saw the marks on the metal, you know. I can't imagine the horror those men went through in their final moments."

"This is irrelevant," he added as his voice was once again commandeered by the figure. "Mistakes have been made by all parties, but a line must be drawn in the sand or the suffering will go on forever. One of you hurt us many years ago, and she went unpunished. That was wrong, and now we demand redress. Will you do the right thing?"

"I -"

"Or must I show you what will happen if you do not?"

Before he could get another word out, Joe heard a crashing sound nearby; he turned and looked over his shoulder, just in time to see a shape lumbering between two trees. At first this shape looked human, but after a few paces it stopped and looked round, and in the snowy moonlight Joe saw that its body was twisted and contorted, with bulging muscles struggling to remain attached to bones that – in places – were exposed to the cold night air. The creature, half man and half wolf, stopped for a moment to lean against a tree, and a few seconds later it managed a mournful wailing sound that seemed poised at any moment to become a growl.

Horrified by the sight, Joe stepped back against the rocks.

"It doesn't see you," he said, his voice dripping with pure terror. "I have made sure of that. If it saw you, it would have torn you to pieces by now."

"What... what is it?" he gasped.

"It is the consequence of our error," he added. "Nothing can be done to save it, we can only try to keep it contained during its slow and agonizing death. And we *will* keep it contained, just so long as we are given no reason to abandon our duty. Do you understand now? Our duty is to care for this monstrosity while it dies, and your duty is to punish the one who created the pain in the first place. And you must do that swiftly, because our patience is not endless."

"Get it away from me," Joe stammered as he once more regained control of his own voice. "It's hideous!"

"We know," he said, replying to himself,

"yet it is one of us, or at least it was, and for that reason we cannot murder it. But if you do not get your own house in order, we might be minded to unleash this thing on your town."

"No!"

"Yes, if necessary. Do what needs doing, and do it soon, or what happened to those people on the bus will seem like nothing compared to the horrors we shall have to unleash. Your predecessors were always able to accommodate our demands, we had a good relationship with them. We very much hope that this will continue."

"But -"

Suddenly the creature turned and looked toward Joe, sniffing the air as its one good eye twitched; it seemed to almost notice him, before letting out a stifled cry and stumbling away, bumping against the trees as it disappeared into the distance. Joe, meanwhile, felt a huge sense of relief as he slid down onto the icy ground, watching the half-human, half-wolf creature fading away into the darkness. Even once the beast was gone, however, Joe felt as if his legs were too weak to allow him to stand; his entire body was shaking with fear and he felt as if he'd just had a very close call with death itself.

"You know what you have to do," he whispered finally, before turning to see that the other figure had stepped back into the darkness.

"Do it before -"

Letting out a shocked gasp, he leaned forward as he regained full control over his own voice. Coughing and spluttering, he wiped the back of his hand against his lips and saw specks of blood; he struggled for a few seconds to catch his breath, but as he remained sitting on the cold ground he already knew that he had no choice, that he had to take action to maintain a wider peace. In that sense, no individual life mattered very much at all; instead, he told himself to focus on the bigger picture and on the safety and security of Sobolton as a whole.

"I know," he said softly, his voice filled with a growing sense of dread. "Damn it, I know exactly what I have to do."

CHAPTER ELEVEN

Today...

"NO?" JOHN SAID, RAISING a skeptical eyebrow as he stood behind his desk. "What do you mean?"

"I mean," Joe replied, struggling to catch his breath a little, "that whatever you think you're doing by poking around in that old bus, you need to leave it alone. What happened was a terrible accident but there's no point digging it all up. Now, I fully understand that Susan Walpole and the other widows wanted to know about the three men who weren't found in the wreckage, but so much time has gone by, it's just a complete waste of time trying to figure that out."

"I was only going over the old case files," John said. "As a courtesy."

"I should have known this would happen," Joe muttered, limping over to the window and looking out for a moment at the street. "People thought they could capitalize on the arrival of a new sheriff by asking him to dig into all sorts of past events. Half this town lives in the past, John, and I'm sure soon there'll be more of them lining up at your door, asking you to investigate things that happened ten, twenty, thirty or more years ago. You need to focus on the present."

"What -"

"How's it going with that Little Miss Dead girl?"

"I'm working on it."

"So you haven't made any progress, huh?"

"I'm working on it," John said again.

"Don't kid a kidder," Joe replied, turning to him and then pausing for a moment as if studying his face. "It was quite a peculiar chain of events that ended up with you becoming the new sheriff, John, but I came around to seeing the positives. The people of Sobolton wanted fresh blood, they wanted someone from far away, someone who they believed could look at the town with fresh eyes." He began to make his way slowly back over to the desk. "I happen to think they were misguided, but I understand where they were coming from. The point is, there are positives and negatives to you being an outsider."

"I'm doing my very best to serve the people of this town," John said firmly. "In the case of the bus, Doctor Law came to me and -"

"Robert Law's a crank," Joe sighed, rolling his eye theatrically. "I never liked the man. He's got that local charm that people go on about, but the man's a troublemaker. I learned to mostly ignore him, and you should too. Take his reports and read 'em, I'm not denying that he's good at his job, but ignore all the other crap that comes out of his mouth."

"I'll take your advice onboard," John said cautiously.

"Do you want to know what really happened to the three men who initially survived the bus crash?" Joe asked, lowering his voice a little. "I'll tell you. Something got to them, probably wolves, and hauled them out of the wreckage and most likely ate them alive. They would have suffered agonizing deaths, deaths that we shouldn't try to imagine even if we could. I heard wolves go for the bellies first, ripping the guts out, so the men would have known exactly what was happening to them. Now, do you want to go to Susan Walpole and explain that to her? Or do you want to do what I did, and say you can't be sure what really happened, and let her think there's some mystery."

"Do you have any proof that they were killed by wolves?"

"It's pretty goddamn obvious, John. Even an idiot should be able to figure it out. But if you want to go to that poor old woman and tell her the truth, then by all means, be my guest. Let her imagine the horror, let her know that her husband – the man she'd been married to for a matter of hours – probably died screaming in agony as those animals dug though his intestines. Let her know all of that, and then come back and tell me how the truth works."

He hesitated, before turning and heading to the door.

"What wolves?" John asked.

Stepping out into the corridor, Joe turned to him.

"I thought there were no wolves in the local area," John continued. "Apart from a few random strays every now and again, that is."

"If you want to last round these parts," Joe said cautiously, "you need to learn what to focus on and what to ignore. And you need to learn fast."

***

"That doesn't surprise me one bit," Robert Law muttered, clearly irritated as he sat in a booth at the diner. "Joe Hicks was always a jumped-up little wannabe Hitler with delusions of grandeur. He thought being sheriff meant he was basically the king of Sobolton."

"Why exactly did he quit?" John asked as he set his hat down on the table.

"He was forced out," Robert explained. "I guess eventually people just got sick of feeling like they were being lied to all the time. That, and there were some financial irregularities that he could no longer hide, things to do with the budget. The people demanded someone new, and Joe resisted for the longest time, but eventually he agreed to step down provided the new appointment had to be someone not from the local area. He went from resisting the idea of an outsider to positively demanding one."

"Why would he specify that?"

"Pride, probably," Robert said with a sigh. "He thought he'd be able to step in an influence his replacement, which it seems is exactly what he's doing right now." He paused for a moment. "I've always been of the opinion that Joe Hicks knows more about what happened to the survivors of that bus crash."

"There are marks on the metal that seem consistent with some kind of..."

John's voice trailed off.

"Say it," Robert continued. "No matter how stupid it might sound."

"Some kind of animal attack," John told him. "It'd have to be something pretty strong to have left those marks in solid metal, but I imagine it's not beyond the bounds of possibility. It might have been more than one. And I think probably part of what Joe told me was correct, I think something most likely *did* take the men who'd survived. What I don't understand is why Joe would go to such extreme efforts to cover that fact up. And how come there have been no scraps of the men found? Not even bone?"

"Or Joe covered up any evidence."

"To save the feelings of the widows?"

"A convenient excuse," Robert replied. "You know, men can become addicted to secrecy just like they can become addicted to any substance. You start lying about enough things, eventually you end up lying all the time, because you can't even remember any other way of talking." He paused for a moment. "I've got high hopes for you, though. You seem like a straightforward kind of guy. Are you much into fishing?"

"As much as the next man."

"The fishing round Sobolton's crazy," Robert continued, clearly warming to his theme. "Even in this weather, if you know what you're doing, the rewards can be spectacular. One day, when we've both got a spare second, I'll take you out to this spot I know where the going's like nothing else you've ever experienced. I invited Joe Hicks fishing once, but he turned me down flat. I know I'm biased and I'm probably completely wrong, but I've never trusted a man who doesn't like fishing. I just feel like that tells you everything you need to know about a man's character. Or a woman, for that matter."

"That sounds like fun," John said, before hearing a buzzing sound and pulling his phone from his pocket. He glanced at the screen, then he gestured to Robert to wait a moment as he answered. "Tommy, I'm just over at the diner. What's up?"

He listened, and after a few seconds he glanced at Robert again before getting to his feet.

"Okay," he said cautiously, "I'm on my way now. I'll bring Doctor Law with me."

"What is it?" Robert asked as John cut the call.

"The station just received a call from the retirement facility down the road," John said cautiously. "Susan Walpole went out this morning and she hasn't been seen since. Her cellphone has been switched off, and they're worried something might have happened to her."

"She's gone out to Henge Cliff again," Robert muttered as he stood up and stepped around the table. "Damn it, I should have kept an eye on her. I should have known she'd go out there again."

"Is there nowhere else she might be?" John asked.

"I know that woman better than I know anyone else in this entire town," Robert said firmly. "She's gone back out there, John, and in this weather she's in real danger. Not that she likely cares too much. She doesn't have long left, and I'm pretty sure she's determined to either find the truth about her dead husband or die trying."

CHAPTER TWELVE

Twenty years earlier...

"IT'S ALL SORTED. LISTEN, I know you have your doubts, Joe, but you have to believe me... I fixed it. All of it. Lisa's not going to cause any more trouble. She's back on the right path."

As he sat in his car, staring out at Lisa's apartment on the other side of the road, Joe Hicks couldn't help but think back to his conversations with Rod Sondnes. He and Rod had been good friends, they'd understood one another on an instinctual level, and there had been times when they'd even been able to communicate without necessarily talking; Joe had been able to guess what Rod was thinking, and vice versa, and their friendship had been put to the ultimate test when

Rod's daughter Lisa had gotten herself into one hell of a mess.

"As long as you're sure, Rod," Joe remembered replying. "If it was anyone else, I'd have to take matters into my own hands, but if you're really sure that you've got this sorted out."

"I'm sure," Rod had insisted. "I just got off the phone with the doctor. It's already done."

Now, as those words faded away into the mists of time, Joe saw a familiar figure heading along the sidewalk. Lisa was on her way home with some shopping bags, trudging through the snow; for a moment he was struck by her perseverance, and also by a sense of profound loneliness as he watched her starting to sort through her pockets for her keys. He knew that Lisa was a successful veterinarian, but he also knew that her personal life had always been something of a mess and that she'd struggled to make connections. She was a pretty enough woman, he told himself, albeit not one who ever seemed to glam herself up. At least she'd had her relationship with Wade Rogers for a while, although that had ended in regrettable circumstances.

He watched as she struggled with her keys for a moment, and then as she slipped through the front door and disappeared from sight.

"Damn it, Lisa," he said finally, his voice filled with a kind of weary resignation. "Why couldn't you just stay out of trouble?"

***

"Damn it, Lisa," she muttered under her breath as she pushed some bags of potato chips into the cupboard, "why can't you just stay out of trouble?"

Swinging the cupboard door shut, she wandered back to the counter and grabbed her now-empty bags, before scrunching them up and carrying them to the hallway. She took a moment to shove the bags back into her jacket pockets, and then she examined the torn patch on the jacket's shoulder. She knew she should get the damage repaired, or maybe even shell out for a new jacket entirely, but after a moment's inspection she satisfied herself that the damage was mostly cosmetic. Besides, she only ever wore it to go out into the wild, so she wasn't exactly trying to impress anyone.

Speaking of which, she checked her watch; she had to be out at Mike Dingle's farm a few hours later to check on his herd, but she figured she had a little time first.

Heading through to the front room, she told herself that there was no point spending money on a new jacket when the old one was still perfectly functional. And as she flopped down in the armchair, she reminded herself that she still needed to keep plenty of money back until the claim was sorted on her car.

Reaching for the book she'd left next to the chair, she set it on her lap and opened to the page where she'd left off. The story was some absurd nonsense about killer lobsters, something she wouldn't usually bother to read at all, although she'd found herself getting sucked into the drama; she looked down at the opening to the next chapter and tried to focus, but she could feel her eyes trying to close and after a few seconds she leaned back and took a deep breath. Finally she closed her eyes just for a moment, telling herself that she could rest without sleeping; the moment began to drag on, and although she knew she was on the verge of dozing, Lisa wasn't quite able to force herself to wake up.

And slowly, without warning, in her mind's eye she began to see what appeared to be some sort of cabin in a clearing, with trees all around. The cabin wasn't very big, but there were a few steps leading up to the front door and somehow she felt that she'd seen this place before.

Suddenly her eyes snapped open and she froze as she heard a distinct bumping sound coming from her bedroom. She'd been half asleep but now she felt wide awake, and sure enough she heard another bumping sound.

She remained completely still, worried that someone might have broken into the apartment. As her heart started racing, she began to slowly get to her feet while glancing around for something she might be able to use as a weapon. Spotting the rifle leaning against a nearby wall, she picked it up and – although she knew it wasn't loaded – she told herself that she could at least use the damn thing to threaten any intruder.

"Hello?" she called out, looking along the corridor that led to the bedroom, where the door had been left open. "Is anyone there?"

She waited.

Silence.

"If there's anyone there," she continued, trying to sound as tough and confident as possible, "you need to know that I'm armed. Okay? I've got a gun and I'm not afraid to use it."

Again, she heard only silence.

"I've actually used it before," she added, thinking back to the creature on the icy road before reminding herself that she had to stay focused on the present. Adjusting her grip on the rifle, she took a couple of steps forward. "This is a really bad idea," she continued, "but it doesn't have to end badly, not if you simply come out right now with your hands up. Do you understand?"

Still watching the bedroom door, she listened out for even the slightest hint of a presence. She was trying to remember whether or not she'd closed the door to the bedroom before leaving that morning; quickly realizing that she was never going to come up with an answer, she started slowly making her way along the corridor even as she knew that she might be making a terrible mistake.

Reaching the door, she kept the gun raised as she backed against the opposite wall. She aimed through the doorway, but to her relief she saw no sign of anyone so far.

"You're making a big mistake if you think you can mess with me," she said firmly. "Just because I'm a woman living alone, that doesn't mean I'll cower and quake. If you don't show yourself right now, I'll be perfectly justified in shooting you."

Hoping that her words might draw any intruder out, she hesitated before hurrying into the room. She checked behind the door, then she checked under the bed, and finally she got to her feet and realized that she might have been wrong all along. She felt sure that the sound had come from the bedroom, but now there was no sign of anyone at all and she began to realize that she was feeling pretty jumpy.

Checking her watch, she saw that the time was a little after one in the afternoon. She'd only popped home to grab a few things on her lunch break, and she knew that more than anything she needed to get back to the office.

Stepping back out of the bedroom, she

listened for a moment longer before gently bumping the door shut.

"Stupid," she said under her breath as she carried the rifle back to the front room, briefly propping it against the wall again before hiding it in the cupboard instead. "There's no need to get paranoid, Lisa."

Worried that she might fall asleep again if she sat down, she instead headed to the door. She briefly wondered about the cabin she'd begun to dream about, before telling herself that there was no point trying to untangle random images thrown up by her brain on the verge of sleep. After checking her pockets and finding no sign of her keys, she glanced around and quickly spotted them resting on the counter; she hurried over and picked them up, only for a small cloud of tiny white flakes to fall away onto the floor.

Crouching down, Lisa, used one fingertip to wipe up some of the flakes. She'd been finding them occasionally for a while now, and she was starting to really wonder where they came from; peering more closely at the flakes, she couldn't shake the sense that they appeared to be small pieces of dry skin, although she was fairly sure that they couldn't have come from her own body. She briefly considered tasting them, before deciding that this would be a step too far. Instead, telling herself that she could try to solve the mystery another time, she brushed the flakes from her finger and then stood up, before heading to the door as she began to run through a mental list of her afternoon tasks.

Once she was gone, the apartment stood in silence for several minutes before finally a faint bumping sound emerged from the bedroom.

CHAPTER THIRTEEN

Today...

"OKAY, I NEED THIS section of the forest searched immediately!" John called out, reaching the foot of the path that led down to the base of Henge Cliff, where half a dozen police officers had assembled in the snow. "We have reason to believe that Susan Walpole came to this spot, and that she might be searching the forest."

"There's no sign of any tracks," Tommy told him.

"I know," he continued, "but there are plenty of spaces where the canopy has kept the snow away, so she still might have come this way. I want to remind all of you that Mrs. Walpole is a frail and vulnerable woman with health and mobility issues. She can't be out in this cold weather for too long, especially if she's not suitably attired. If you find her, your priority has to be getting her back to safety. There'll be time to ask questions later. Is that understood?"

A murmur of agreement spread through the assembled ranks.

"Let's move, people," John continued, waving a gloved hand to indicate that they needed to spread out. "I'm sure you all know that this is an extremely time-sensitive operation."

"I don't like this," Robert muttered, stepping over to join John as the officers began to make their way out between the trees. "She's had time to get quite a head-start. Even if she's not moving fast, we might never find her."

"I'm sure there'll be some kind of indication of her location soon," John replied. "As far as we know she's not actively trying to cover her tracks or -"

"Stop trying to make me feel better!" Robert snapped. "I'm not an idiot, I know exactly how much danger she's in! In case it had slipped your mind, I'm a doctor! I know what you cops are like when you're trying to sugarcoat the bad news, but I'd appreciate it if you'd respect me enough to be honest!"

"I'm sorry."

"No, *I'm* sorry," Robert said with a heavy

sigh, before looking down at his walking stick. "The truth is, I'm frustrated because I know I won't be any use out there. I'll only slow you down, John, so it's best if I wait here. After all, there's always a chance that she might come back this way. Someone should be here."

"I'll let you know as soon as we hear anything."

"You have to find her, John," Robert continued, his voice filling with a growing sense of desperation. "She's a good woman. The best. I can't bear to think of her alone out here in the cold, potentially..."

His voice trailed off for a moment.

"Please find her," he added finally. "Before it's too late."

***

"So what do we think Mrs. Walpole's doing out here, again?" Tommy asked a few minutes later, as he and John picked their way between the trees, their feet stepping alternately on patches of snow and swatches of dark frozen mud. "Seems like an odd day to go for a walk."

"She's searching for her dead husband," John replied, still looking around in case he spotted any sign of the missing woman. He could hear his officers calling her name in the distance. "Robert has been extremely sensitive and careful when discussing the situation, but reading between the lines I think he's worried about her state of mind."

"Do you think she has dementia?"

"I think *something's* not right," John admitted.

They walked on for a few seconds, lost in silence, although John still couldn't quite shake the feeling that he was out of his depth. The more he tried to understand Sobolton, the more he felt as if he was bashing his head against a brick wall, and he felt somehow as if he was less sure of his own beliefs. He'd already seen a wolf-like creature fall through the ice of a frozen lake, and he'd seen visions of a ghostly little girl, and he'd even become tangentially involved in a truly bizarre incident involving a madman and a bunch of swans; any one of those events would have been shocking enough on their own, but together they constituted an avalanche of insanity and now he felt as if he was on the verge of adding another strange tale to his burgeoning collection of experiences.

Something was going to have to give.

"Okay, what's the deal?" he asked finally.

"What do you mean?"

"This town," he continued, as he ducked down to avoid a low-hanging branch. "Don't tell me you're not aware of it, because I know that can't be true. Everyone in Sobolton has to be aware that things just... aren't quite right."

"Aren't most small towns weird in their own ways?" Tommy suggested.

"Not like this," John said firmly. "I keep thinking the swan stuff must have been a dream. I actually half expect to wake up and find I suffered a blow to the head, and the whole Wentworth Stone thing was some kind of hallucination."

"That *was* kind of nuts," Tommy admitted. "Even by Sobolton standards."

"So do people round here just ignore it?" John asked. "Is that the solution? Do they just pretend like it's not happening, and they go about their lives just trying to zone it all out? Is that the only way to live in this place?"

"It's not a bad way to go about things," Tommy replied.

"But you notice things, don't you?" John continued. "Sometimes I feel like there's this big secret that everyone's trying to keep, and as the person who's ultimately responsible for keeping the town safe, that's kind of a problem."

"There's no big secret," Tommy told him. "It's more the case that people... choose not to ask."

"Because they're scared?"

"Joe used to mention things occasionally," Tommy continued. "That's why I never really questioned him too much or got suspicious about what he was doing. I could tell that he was aware of things, heavy things that weighed him down. If you want my honest opinion, I'm pretty sure that occasionally he even had to do things he didn't want to do." He paused as they made their way a little further through the forest. "Truthfully, that's why I didn't go for the job of sheriff when Joe announced he was retiring. I know everyone wanted an outsider, but Tracy still thought I could've changed their minds if I'd really wanted it."

"But you didn't?"

"I didn't want to know whatever Joe knew," he explained. "I'm sorry if that makes me sound stupid, but I just don't. I don't want that responsibility. I'm..."

His voice trailed off for a few seconds.

"Well," he continued finally, "if you want to know the truth of it, I'm scared of knowing too much."

"About Sobolton?"

"Sometimes about Sobolton," he replied, "but sometimes about the whole world. Like... all of it. I just feel like there's so much badness out there, and so much evil, and to face it all would be soul-destroying. I've got my wife and my son, and my home, and my job, and I'm sort of content with all of that. I know the real, true bad stuff is out there, and I just pray every night that it'll never get to me. It shouldn't, should it? Not if I keep my head down, at least."

"That's definitely one way of living," John told him.

"I know I'm a coward."

"I didn't say you were a coward," John replied. "I think everyone has to find their own way to navigate a path through the world, and sometimes that means -"

Before he could finish, his right foot pressed down hard against something that crunched into the forest floor. Stopping and looking down, John saw some kind of plastic band with a small device attached; he picked the device up and turned it around, and he immediately realized that he knew exactly what he'd found. Turning, he looked all around, but he saw no sign of anything untoward anywhere else in the forest.

"What is it?" Tommy asked.

"A medical alert bracelet from the same facility that reported Susan Walpole missing," John explained, holding it up so that he could get a better look not only at the device itself but also at the torn band. "It's been ripped, as if someone pulled it off."

"Do you think it belongs to Mrs. Walpole?"

"We have to assume that she came this way," John replied, still looking round in case there was any further sign of the missing woman. "Call the other teams and tell them to head in this direction. If we don't find Susan before sundown, there's no way she could survive a night out in the elements. We need to find her before the worst happens."

CHAPTER FOURTEEN

Twenty years earlier...

"THIS IS ALL LOOKING perfectly good to me," Lisa said, sounding a little breathless as she got to her feet and stepped back from the rear of the cow. "The pregnancy's advancing exactly as we'd expect, and I don't think the cold weather's having any adverse impact."

"You don't think she seems a little off?" Mike asked.

"I think she looks pretty good for an expectant mother," she replied, patting the cow's side, eliciting a grumbling moo in the process. "As a nonseasonal polyestrus, she's wired to handle all sorts of conditions." She headed over to the table in the corner of the barn, where she began to wash her hands and arms, scraping away as much excrement as possible. "You were right to call me out, though. If you're worried, it's always better to get these things checked."

"My old man used to go on and on about instinct," Mike muttered. "He told me that was a farmer's most valuable asset. He had it, but I'm not sure that I do."

"How long have you been running the farm for?"

"Almost three years," he told her. "Three years in the summer."

"That's not long," she pointed out with a faint smile as she scrubbed her left forearm. "I visit some people who've been doing the same job for three decades, and they still wouldn't claim to know everything. In fact, if someone *did* say they knew everything, that's when I'd start to worry. I'm sure your instinct's just fine."

"It's just hard being in the old man's shadow," Mike admitted, before hesitating for a moment. "Then again, I guess you know about that sort of thing. Sorry, I hope I'm not stepping on any toes there."

"Not at all," she told him, grabbing a towel and starting to dry her arms as she wandered to the wide open door and looked out across the snowy fields. "You've got good land here, Mike. I know people tried to buy it off your father a few times."

"Someone tried to buy it from me just last year."

"You didn't want to sell?"

"I couldn't," he explained, making his way over to join her. "I'd feel like I was betraying him. He never asked me if I wanted to run the place after him, it was all just kinda assumed. On my part as well as his. I don't think I ever seriously entertained the idea of doing anything else." He looked out at the falling snow for a moment. "How about you? Did you ever harbor any thoughts of another line of work?"

"It was always this," she admitted. "I don't -"

Stopping suddenly, she spotted a light in the distance, a single spot in the otherwise dark forest that ran across the horizon. Assuming that she must be imagining things, she squinted a little to get a better look, but after a few seconds she realized that something seemed to be out there.

"Do you see that light?" she asked, pointing toward the trees.

"Where?"

"Over there," she continued. "There's nothing that should be causing that, is there?"

"I don't see a light," he murmured, "but no, there's nothing out that way but mile after mile of forest."

"Directly above the old fence post," she

replied, "the one that's leaning by itself, there's a light in the trees. It's small, maybe just a single beam, but I definitely see something. It doesn't seem to be moving, either."

"If you say so," Mike chuckled. "I don't see it, but I'm not gonna argue with you." Hearing some mooing from over his shoulder, he turned to look at the cows. "They seem more settled now," he continued. "It's almost as if they saw you washing yourself clean and they realized that means you'll be leaving soon. Cows are smart, so I wouldn't put it past them."

"Neither would I," she replied, still keeping her eyes fixed on the light in the distance. "That goes for a lot of animals. You underestimated some of them at your peril."

***

"Remember to call me if you have any more concerns!" Lisa called back to Mike a short while later, as she made her way around to the other side of her rental car. "I'll be in touch next month!"

Climbing into the car, she pulled the door shut and took a moment to rub her hands together for warmth. As she looked out through the windshield, she saw the distant trees again, and once more she was struck by the sight of a light somewhere far off in the darkness. Mike had claimed not to be able to see the light at all, which she figured was strange, and she couldn't help wondering what could possibly be happening out there in the forest. She told herself that there were all sorts of possibilities, and that it was really none of her business, and finally she began to pull the belt across her chest.

Suddenly, in the blink of an eye, she saw a lonely cabin in a clearing, with a single candle burning in one of the windows. The vision was so strong and so insistent in her mind, that for a few seconds – even with her eyes wide open – she could see nothing else. Finally she let out a gasp and leaned back in her seat, and the vision faded.

Staring out at the distant forest again, still seeing the light, Lisa tried to work out what the cabin could possibly mean. She'd seen it twice now in brief, fleeting glimpses that seemed to have burst from her subconscious mind; there had been so much detail in the image, however, that she felt it had to be real. She also knew, deep down, that there was a great sense of familiarity attached to the place. She'd been there before, even if she couldn't remember when or why or how.

Taking a deep breath, she told herself to stay calm. After just a few more seconds, however, she realized that the cabin was returning to her thoughts. Whereas previously the strange vision had appeared in a flash, now it seemed to be very slowly creeping into her mind, edging closer and closer to the front and refusing to fade even as she blinked. She could see the dirty wooden facade, and the steps leading up to the decrepit front door, and somehow she was also able to see the cramped little room on the door's other side. In that moment she realized that she knew every inch of the cabin, inside and out, and that somehow she'd definitely been there before.

In her mind's eye, she approached the steps and made her way up to the door. She reached out for the handle and felt its cold metal against her hand; the illusion seemed almost more real than anything else, and as she turned the handle she couldn't shake a growing sense of fear that had begun to fill her chest.

Pushing the door open, she saw only darkness inside. Despite her terror, she stepped forward, entering what seemed to be a void. She could feel slightly springy floorboards beneath her feet, but otherwise there seemed to be no 'there' to the inside of the cabin, as if there were no walls and no ceiling. Reaching out, she ran a hand through the darkness, determined to find something – anything – to feel. Discovering nothing, she instinctively took a step forward even though she knew she was risking everything, and then she stepped forward again and again, walking slowly through the void. And then, looking over her shoulder, she realized that the door was gone.

Not shut.

Not out of sight.

Just gone.

"Hello?" she whispered, still trying to work out when she'd been in the cabin before. "Is anyone here? My name -"

Stopping herself just in time, she realized somehow that her name was already known in this place. She turned and looked all around in the darkness, and now she was able to sense someone staring back at her, even if she was unable to see anything at all. She reached out again, trying not to panic, and then she turned and hurried back the way she'd just come, desperately trying to find the door. Once she'd taken several steps, she realized that she should have reached the door by now or at least thudded into a wall; she continued to walk in a straight line, and she heard her footsteps against the wooden floor, but there was no sign of the actual room itself.

"Hello?" she said again, as she felt a growing sense of panic rising through her chest. "What -"

"Lisa?"

Startled, she spun around, and in that second she suddenly felt the seat of the car beneath her. The belt pulled tight against her chest, and the darkness faded to nothing, replaced by the cold car. She blinked a couple of times, trying to get her head straight, before letting out a shocked gasp as someone knocked on the window. Seeing Mike staring in at her, she took a moment to pull her thoughts together and then she wound the window down.

"Hey," she said, trying to seem normal.

"Are you okay?" he asked. "I was doing stuff in the back, and then I came out and saw you still sitting here. Have you been here ever since you left?"

"What -"

Realizing that night had begun to fall, Lisa realized that she must have been sitting in the car all alone for several hours. She opened her mouth to tell Mike that she wasn't sure what had happened, but at the last second she held back as she told herself that she really needed to avoid coming across badly.

"I'm fine," she stammered finally. "It's all good. I'm sorry, I didn't mean to bother you. I was just running through some thoughts in my head." She forced a smile. "That's all."

CHAPTER FIFTEEN

Today...

"SUSAN!" A VOICE CALLED out in the distance, echoing through the forest. "Susan Walpole!"

"Susan!" Tommy yelled, standing right next to John as they stopped in a clearing. "Susan Walpole, can you hear me?"

"She can't have gone this far," John muttered, unable to hide the sense of frustration in his voice. "Sure, she got a head-start, but she can't exactly have been moving fast, not at her age. We should have found her by now."

"Maybe the woman of the forest got her."

"The who?"

John turned to Tommy and immediately saw a troubled expression on the other man's face.

"Oh, it's just a local legend," Tommy explained. "It's total nonsense, there are just some people who claim an evil woman lives in the forest in a pit and..."

His voice trailed off.

"Well," he continued, "I don't see that it's relevant right now."

"Yeah, I doubt that it is," John replied cautiously. "Let's just stick to the facts for now, okay? It's getting dark and Mrs. Walpole isn't going to last long as the temperature keeps dropping. You can't think of anywhere in the area where she might be taking shelter, can you?"

"There's nothing," Tommy told him.

"No old ranger huts, anything like that?"

"Nope," Tommy continued. "Not remotely nearby, at least."

"Then we have to assume that she's still outside," John pointed out, before examining the broken alert bracelet again. "These things are strong. They're designed so that they're impossible to take off without a key, but look at the frayed edges. Something ripped this apart."

"Do you think Mrs. Walpole did that?"

"I'm not sure she could have, even if she'd wanted to," he replied, before taking an even closer look at the torn bracelet. "Doesn't it look kind of... chewed to you?"

"I guess," Tommy admitted. "Do you think

Mrs. Walpole chewed her own bracelet off?"

"I think -"

Before John could finish, they both heard a woman crying out. More of a startled yelp than a scream, the sound was over almost before it had begun, but John and Tommy immediately set off to the east, hurrying down a frozen slope at such speed that they both had to reach out and steady themselves against passing trees.

"Do you think that was her?" Tommy asked breathlessly.

"Unless there are any other women lost in the forest this afternoon," John replied, "I think it's a safe -"

Suddenly he lost his footing, letting out a gasp as he slipped and fell hard against the ground. Unable to grab onto anything, he slithered down the slope before finally coming to a stop at the bottom, hitting a frozen stump and gasping again as he felt the air getting knocked out of his lungs.

"Sir, are you okay?" Tommy asked, hurrying after him.

"I'm fine!" John hissed, more embarrassed than hurt as he slowly got to his feet, covered in snowy half-frozen mud. Wincing, he started brushing himself down. "I'm sorry, I'm just not used to the rugged terrain round these parts. Believe it or not, I don't have much experience on ice."

"You'll get used to it," Tommy told him.

"We all do."

"Where did that cry come from?" John asked, stepping carefully around the stump as he continued to brush dirt from the sleeve of his jacket. "It must have been somewhere round here, right?"

"I think so," Tommy replied, before looking up at the darkening sky. "Sir, in about an hour and a half, two hours at most, the sun's gonna go down and I really don't think we're going to have much luck then."

"What are you suggesting?"

"I'm suggesting that we need some other plan," Tommy said plaintively, as if he was struggling to figure out exactly what that plan might entail. "I'm sorry, I know I'm not being a whole ton of use right now, am I? I just worry that we're going to end up chasing round and round in circles." He paused, before furrowing his brow. "She belongs out here," he added. "She's been taken by the forest now."

"What do you mean?" John asked.

"I... don't know why I just said that," Tommy replied, before shaking his head. "Sir, I'm sorry, I think I just had some kind of brain-fart." He winced suddenly. "It's weird, I've got a bit of a headache. Sorry, I'll try to pull myself together."

"Susan Walpole can't be far away," John pointed out, as he examined the sleeve of his jacket and found a small rip. "I don't care how dark it gets,

I have a flashlight and I'm not giving up until she's safe and well. And that's an order that applies to everyone else out here as well. We came here to find this woman, and we're not stopping until the job's done."

"Of course," Tommy replied, touching the side of his head as he followed John through the forest.

"Mrs. Walpole!" John called out, as other voices shouted variations of the same thing in the distance. "This is the Sobolton Sheriff's Department! We just want to take you home and make sure that you're alright! If you can hear me, can you give me some kind of sign?"

"You won't find her," Tommy muttered. "Not until we let you."

"What was that?"

"Nothing," Tommy added, wincing again as he felt another ripple of pain running through his head. "I'm sorry, Sir, I don't know what came over me. To be honest, I'm feeling a little spaced out."

"Mrs. Walpole!" John shouted. "If -"

Before he could finish, another shriek rang out in the distance, sounding a little more troubled than earlier.

"That has to be her!" John said firmly, picking up the pace as he hurried through the forest, still using the trees on either side for support. "Mrs. Walpole!" he shouted. "Keep making a noise and we'll try to find you! Mrs. Walpole, I -"

Suddenly she cried out again, and as he stopped to get his bearings John spotted a flash of white in the distance as a figure ran through a clearing.

"There!" he yelled, setting off after her as the figure hurried away. "Mrs. Walpole, wait! We're only trying to help!"

"Uh, Mrs. Walpole?" Tommy called out, struggling to keep up with John now. "Would you mind stopping?"

"What's wrong with her?" John muttered. "She must have heard us, but she's going in the wrong direction."

"She's certainly moving fast," Tommy pointed out. "Something must have given her a scare."

"I'm almost losing sight of her," John admitted, before hearing another cry that suddenly stopped dead, accompanied by a rustling sound. "Wait, I think she might have fallen!"

For the next couple of minutes they pushed on, still trying desperately to locate the missing woman. They stopped a couple of times, trying to figure out which way to go next, but there was no sign of the figure in white now and – as he reached the crest of a small hill – John looked around and began to worry that they'd lost sight of her entirely. And then, just as he was about to suggest to Tommy that they should head in a different direction, he spotted something white moving down at the bottom of the hill, struggling to get up from a mass of snow and dirt.

"Found her!" John gasped, immediately starting to pick his way down the hill, almost slipping several times but just about managing to stay on his feet. "Hurry!"

Reaching the bottom, John scrambled over to the spot where Susan Walpole – wearing nothing but a thin nightshirt that was torn in several places – was still trying and mostly failing to stand. Seemingly unaware that anyone had been after her, she let out a shocked gasp as soon as John touched her arm; spinning round to face him, she seemed briefly unsure about what was happening, and then she turned and looked away between the trees.

"Mrs. Walpole, we've been searching everywhere for you," John said, as he saw small scratches all over her hands. "What are you doing out here?"

"I came looking for my dear Timothy," she stammered, as tears filled her eyes. "I was looking for him and the two other men who were never found after the crash. I heard them calling out to me and I tried to follow their voices."

"Okay, let's get you back to town," John said, removing his jacket and placing it over her shoulders. "We have to be -"

"You don't understand," she replied, turning to him as tears ran down her cheeks. "I came looking for them, Sheriff Tench. And finally, after all these years, I found them!"

CHAPTER SIXTEEN

Twenty years earlier...

AS SHE CUT THE engine and climbed out of the rental car, Lisa still couldn't help thinking about the strange cabin that had appeared without warning in her head. Twice now she'd seen the same place, and she still couldn't shake an unsettled fear that somehow she recognized the cabin.

Or, rather, that she *should* recognize it.

Slamming the door shut, she walked carefully across the icy parking lot and headed toward the office door.

"Lisa?"

Startled, she stopped and looked over her shoulder, and she immediately flinched as she saw Wade standing just a few feet away. Dressed in heavy winter gear as usual, he looked more than a little nervous as he stepped toward her, but he was at least trying to wear a smile.

"Hey," he said cautiously, "long time, huh? I bet I'm the last person you expected to see today."

"That's an understatement," she replied, glancing around. "What are you doing in town? I thought you weren't coming back."

"I couldn't just leave without saying goodbye," he told her. "I know we left things pretty badly on the phone, and I also know that was entirely my fault. I handled things abominably and for that I'll always be sorry."

"Yeah, well..."

Her voice trailed off.

"What do you *want*, Wade?" she added.

"I want to talk," he told her. "I want to kind of make things right. I hate feeling like I did you wrong."

"Well, you kinda did," she pointed out, before sighing and shaking her head. "I really don't want to have this conversation right now, okay? I packaged up all your stuff and sent it to the address you gave me, and I just assumed that I'd never have to talk to you again. Shouldn't you be off somewhere starting your new life with Kerry or Katie or whatever her name is?"

"Karen."

"Whatever," she said again, making an

effort to sound particularly uninterested. "I really don't think that we have anything to talk about."

"Can you hear me out?"

"About what?" she snapped, getting close to the end of her tether. "It's over between us, Wade, and I for one don't really feel like conducting an autopsy of our so-called relationship. It was fun while it lasted but it ended, and now we both have to get on with our lives." She waited for him to accept that she was right, but after a few seconds she realized that she perhaps needed to hammer her point home a little harder. "Separately."

"Do you think we can be friends?"

"I don't want to be friends, Wade," she replied, as her phone beeped. Checking the screen, she saw a perfectly-timed message from Rachel asking about some files. "And now, if you don't mind, I need to get back to work. Please don't turn up here again, Wade, okay? We're done."

With that, she turned and headed to the door.

"I came all this way to talk to you!" he called after her. "Lisa, if you change your mind, I'm in room five at the motel! I'll be there tonight and then I'll be gone in the morning. Lisa? If you change your mind will you come and find me?"

As soon as she was inside, Lisa pushed the door shut and leaned back, taking a deep breath.

"Relax," Rachel said, holding her phone up, "there are no files missing. I just saw that creep talking to you and figured you might want a nice easy excuse to get away."

"You figured right," Lisa said, before peering out the window and seeing that Wade had already walked away. "I don't know what he was doing here and I don't care. I just never want to see him again. Not ever."

***

"Now," Joe Hicks said as he sat in his favorite booth at McGinty's, "the way I see it, no-one oughta be telling any other fellow what he can and can't do on his own property. There's a line where the property starts, and that line is sacrosanct."

"Agreed," Harvey Mullern said darkly, nodding as he sat with his beer. "Anything that happens off a man's property, well, that's fair game. But *on* it? Nobody else's business."

"So that's how I always like to run things round here," Joe continued, barely even noticing as the door opened at the other end of the room. "Most people seem to get onboard with it, too, although there are always a few bad eggs who can't play the same tune as the rest of the band."

"Walt Jordan," one of the men at the bar muttered.

"Walt Jordan," Joe said, nodding sagely. "Damn it, my one big regret is that I didn't go and arrest that son of a bitch yet."

"What for?" Harvey asked.

"Anything," Joe snarled. "I can figure something out once I got on his stinking excuse for a farm. That man always pissed me off and -"

Realizing that someone had stopped next to his table, he looked up and saw Wade standing over him.

"We need to talk," Wade said softly.

"Gentlemen," Joe said with a grin, looking at the other men, "would you excuse me for a moment? I must have a little chat with this fine young fellow."

As the others moved away and reassembled at the bar, Wade took a seat opposite Joe. Clearly uncomfortable and worried about being overheard, Wade glanced around, and he seemed to be waiting until he was sure all the others were deeply engrossed in some new conversation.

"I haven't been in here for a while," he told Joe finally, keeping his voice down. "I used to pop in occasionally after my shifts at the hospital. Somehow I can't quite sit here now without remembering the smell of the -"

"It's good to see you again, Wade," Joe said, interrupting him. "Have you had a chance to talk to young Lisa yet?"

"She's not interested."

"Make her interested."

"Joe, I ended things with her pretty brutally," Wade replied, with a hint of desperation in his voice. "Just like you told me to. I did everything you asked, and I got out."

"How's Karen?"

"Karen's as good as she's ever been," Wade said firmly, "but you have to understand something. We're getting married, and she's expecting a kid in a couple of months. I held on for as long as I could with Lisa, but eventually I just had to get out, and you told me that was fine. I remember sitting right here with you and you told me that I'd done my job better than you ever expected, and I was free to end it and leave."

"And I was telling the truth," Joe replied. "You did exceptionally well. I needed someone to keep an eye on Lisa from close up and report back to me, and you certainly did that. The thing is, since you left the scene so to speak, she seems to be... unraveling. That might be a coincidence, or it might not, but I'm thinking you could sort of steady the ship a little."

"I'm done, Joe."

"I don't think you are," Joe said firmly. "You wouldn't like your childhood sweetheart Karen to know how you've been earning your money, would you? She thinks you've been off for months at a time on the rigs, but if she found out about your little double life here in Sobolton -"

"You promised me she'd never find out," Wade replied, cutting him off. "Joe, please, you swore to me that you'd never try to use this against me."

"I'm not asking you to recommit, Wade," Joe continued. "I would never do that. Think of this as a little... coda to the whole operation. I need you to just find out what's going on in Lisa's head. Talk to her. You don't have to climb back into bed with her or anything like that. I'm not asking you to whore yourself out again."

"Joe -"

"I'll pay you for your time," Joe added. "Double the rate from before, just for one night's work. Do it tonight, Wade. Find out what she's thinking. What she's planning. Get into her head, the way that only you can. And then, when you're done, you can sail off into the sunset. Permanently this time. You and your Karen lady can live long and happy lives far away from Sobolton, and nobody ever has to find out about your business with Lisa. Not if you do what I'm asking."

"I knew it," Wade replied through gritted teeth. "When you called me up again out of the blue, I knew you were going to try to blackmail me over this."

"It's not blackmail, it's simply a case of finishing the job that you started." He stared at Wade for a moment, as if really trying to make him understand that he had no choice. "Then we can both be happy," he added finally, "and nobody has to get fed to the wolves."

CHAPTER SEVENTEEN

Today...

"GODDAMN CELLPHONES," ROBERT LAW muttered, holding his phone a little higher as he sat at the foot of Henge Cliff, still trying to get some service. "You'd think they'd invent one that works when you're a little off the beaten track."

He watched the screen for a moment longer, before hearing a huffing and puffing sound coming from nearby. He turned just in time to see the somewhat disheveled figure of Joe Hicks struggling to make his way down the steep slope, and he watched as Joe finally stopped at the bottom and paused to get his breath back.

"What are you doing here?" Joe snapped.

"I could ask you the same question," Robert

pointed out.

"Don't try being smart with me," Joe sneered. "We're not in your office or your morgue now. I asked you a question. What are you doing here?"

"Why is that any of your concern?"

"I -"

"What are you gonna doe, Joe?" Robert continued. "Threaten to arrest me? As far as I'm aware, you don't have that authority anymore, do you?"

"You're treading on thin ice," Joe muttered, clearly annoyed as he began to make his way past, looking out into the forest.

"Do you want to know something?" Robert asked. "All those years working with you, I had to keep things professional but now I guess I can say what I really think."

Joe turned to him.

"You're a toad," Robert said firmly. "You're a barely-human relic of the past, a corrupt cop who never did anything good for this town. Worse, you were a terrible sheriff who – thanks to a combination of malice and incompetence – probably never actually caught a criminal who wasn't already in your pocket. You're a small man, Joe, and only smaller men have ever looked up to you."

"You been waiting to say that for a while?"

Joe asked. "Is that the best you've got? I'd have thought with all your fancy education, Doctor Law, that you'd have saved up some good insults for me, but apparently you can't even manage that. I'd show you how it's done, but to be honest I don't care enough. What I *do* care about, however, is whatever nonsense is going on in this forest. Has that damn fool Tench gone wandering out there?"

"He and some officers are searching for a missing woman."

"And you're keeping guard?"

"Bad leg," Robert pointed out, briefly raising his walking stick. "I'd only have slowed them down."

"I knew this would happen," Joe muttered. "I tried to subtly warn him off, but that Tench man just doesn't have any good sense or instinct. Now he's blundering around, getting mixed up in something that really isn't any of his business, and he has no idea how much trouble he could cause."

"Feeling left out?" Robert replied, raising an amused eyebrow. "Worried that the new guy's gonna show you up? The people of Sobolton might not be so friendly to you, Joe, once they see how a real sheriff operates. John Tench is a good man. He's certainly a much better man than you could ever be."

"It's about the bus, isn't it?" Joe continued. "Damn it, I've been waiting years for the last of those widows to die off. When Doris Warner popped her clogs and that left only Susan Walpole, I figured I was so close now, especially seeing as how Susan's not exactly in the best of health. But Susan had to start acting up, didn't she? That woman was always the most stubborn of them all. I should have found some way to shut her up."

"Why, Joe?" Robert asked. "Why do you want to keep the truth from coming out?"

"Because it was my *job* to keep the truth from coming out," Joe sneered angrily. "Because whether they knew it or not, whether they were willing to admit it or not, that's what the people of Sobolton wanted me to do. Until they got fancy new ideas in their heads and decided they wanted a change. Well, they've got that change, and I'm pretty sure they won't like it, not if he goes storming into situations he doesn't understand."

"And what kind of situation would that be, Joe?" Robert replied. "Cut the enigmatic crap. What really happened on the day that bus came crashing down off the road?"

"With all due respect, Doctor Law," Joe snarled, "it's better if you don't know." He paused, before turning and hurrying between the trees. "I just have to get to that idiot Tench before he messes with the gate."

"*Now* what the hell are you on about?" Robert called after him, trying to follow but giving up almost immediately as his walking stick caught in the snow. "Joe? What do you mean? What gate?"

***

"Just over here," Susan stammered, almost tripping in the snow as she hurried between the trees. "I'm sure of it. They're just here, you'll see them in a moment."

"Mrs. Walpole, I really need you to stop," John said firmly as he and Tommy followed. "Mrs. Walpole? This is the wrong direction. We need to be heading back to -"

"I'm sure it was here," she said, stopping suddenly in a clearing and looking all around. "I'm so sure. Damn it, why can't I remember? I should have left some kind of marker, something to show me the right path."

"Mrs. Walpole," John said, stopping next to her and putting a hand gently on her arm, "I understand your distress in this situation, but I think enough might be enough here. I have a duty to get you to safety." He was shivering a little now, having given Susan his jacket. "The temperature's below zero and you've already been out here for a long time. Doctor Law -"

"There!" Susan gasped, looking past him. "Did you hear it? They're singing! They're calling to me!"

"I didn't hear anything," John told her.

"Listen closely," she continued as fresh tears filled her eyes. "They *want* me to go back to them."

"Mrs. Walpole, I -"

Before he could finish, John felt a cold gust of wind blowing between the trees. He shivered again, but a moment later he realized that the wind was trailing a strange echoing sound, a kind of whistle that seemed to be almost turning into a voice. He turned and followed Susan's gaze, while telling himself that he had to be wrong; he knew most likely he was simply letting Susan's outlandish claims influence his thoughts, but for the next few seconds the whistling wind certainly sounded a lot like a groaning voice.

"Sir," Tommy said cautiously, "I... I don't know, I think... I think maybe I hear something."

"It's them," Susan whispered joyfully, before setting off again between the trees. "I knew you'd hear them too! It's them! They're calling to me!"

"Sir, do you hear it too?" Tommy asked.

"I... hear the wind," John replied, unable to shake a sense of concern as the whistling sound continued. "I'm pretty sure that's all it is."

"And a rattling sound?"

John opened his mouth to ask what Tommy meant, but in that instant he realized that perhaps his deputy was right; somehow, mixed in with the wind and the groaning whistle, a periodic rattling sound was also reaching out through the gloom.

"Let's catch up to her before we lose her again," John said, hurrying after Susan. "It's going to get dark sooner and I really don't want to spend much longer chasing her through the forest. For her own sake, we're going to have to be a little more forceful in getting her back to town."

Ahead, Susan had stopped in another clearing and was staring up at the trees. John caught up to her easily, once again placing a hand on her arm, but once again Susan seemed barely aware that she'd been joined at all.

"Mrs. Walpole," John said firmly, "I -"

"There they are," she whispered as more tears ran down her face. "After so very long, I found them. I always knew that I would."

"That's great," John said, glancing up at the trees before turning to her again, "but I really have to insist that you -"

Stopping suddenly, he took a moment to process what he'd just seen. Slowly turning to look at the trees again, he heard the whistling wind blowing through the forest, rattling the human bones that had been arranged in a series of patterns. Rib-cages, arm and leg bones, even skulls were hanging high up in the branches. As Susan dropped sobbing to her knees in the snow, John could only stare up at the bones as the wind blew a little harder, causing the whistling rattling sound to become louder still.

CHAPTER EIGHTEEN

Twenty years earlier...

"NO, I'LL BE HOME tomorrow," Wade said as he sat on the bed in his motel room, watching the muted television screen while holding a phone against his ear. "Or the day after at the latest. I'm sorry, Karen, but this really will be the last long trip I have to take. At least for a while."

"You said that the last time," Karen replied, her voice sounding a little tinny over the phone's speakers. "Wade, when the baby comes -"

"When the baby comes you won't be able to get rid of me," he said firmly, cutting her off. "I mean it. You're gonna be sick of the sight of me." Glancing at the table next to the bed, he spotted some small white flakes; he reached over and wiped them away. "Believe me, I'm not exactly loving this crumby little motel room. I'd much rather be home with you."

"I love you," she told him.

"And I love you too," he replied. "I just can't wait until our little family is -"

Before he could finish, he heard a gentle knock on the door. He looked across the room and felt a tightening sense of dread in his chest as he realized he could see a figure on the other side of the frosted glass, bathed in the glow from the motel's brightly-lit sign.

"What was that noise?" Karen asked.

"Room service."

"You get room service?" she replied. "It can't be *that* bad at the motel, then. What kind of -"

"I'll call you back later," he said, getting up and taking a moment to straighten himself out in the cracked full-length mirror near the door. "Rest up this evening, yeah? Don't go putting any unnecessary stress on yourself or the baby."

Once he'd cut the call, he took a few more seconds to check himself in the mirror, and then he headed to the door. As soon as he pulled the door open, he found Lisa standing on the step outside, with cars passing behind her on the main road.

"Hey," he said, "what -"

"I need to talk to you," she replied before he could finish. "I'm so sorry, Wade, I know I shouldn't be here but I need to talk to someone or I think I'm going to lose my mind."

"Come in," he said, stepping aside and gesturing for her to enter. "I wasn't sure you'd show up."

"I wasn't planning to," she replied, heading over to the foot of the bed and looking at the silent television for a moment, before turning to him again. "Believe me, when I saw you earlier, I was absolutely certain that I never wanted to see you again."

"I can understand that."

"But you're the only person I can really talk to, Wade," she continued, with a hint of fear in her voice. "That's really screwed-up, I really need to work on getting a few closer friends, because I really shouldn't be having to confide in my ex."

An awkward silence fell between them for a moment.

"It's weird hearing you call me that," he admitted finally. "Your ex."

"I think coming here was a bigger mistake than I realized," she told him, suddenly heading to the door. "I'm sorry, I'm going to leave and -"

"No!" he blurted out, putting his hands on the sides of her arms to stop her, holding her in place. "I mean... please, don't go. I still care for you a huge amount, Lisa, and I want to help you any way that I can." He paused for a moment, before letting go of her arms and finding to his relief that she stayed where she was standing. "There's a vending machine in the reception," he added. "Why don't you wait in here for a few minutes? I'll go and grab us something and then we can talk. Does that sound like a good idea?"

***

"What the hell is this stuff?" Wade muttered a few minutes later, standing in the reception foyer, his face picked out by the lights of the vending machine. "I've never even heard of half this junk."

Crouching down, he peered at the soda bottles at the bottom of the machine, although in truth he was starting to wonder whether he should run to a store and pick up some beer. A moment later, figuring that he might even be able to get some cans at the desk, he got to his feet and headed over to the counter, before leaning over and trying to spot the morose guy who'd checked him into the motel a few hours earlier.

"Hello?" he called out. "Anyone here?"

He waited, but there was no sign of the attendant.

"Hello?" he called out again. "Sorry, I was just wondering whether you sell beer? I've been to a few places in other states where they had a kind of bar and..."

His voice trailed off as he realized that most likely he was barking up the wrong tree. Still, he waited for a few more seconds before tapping the bell on the counter, which he figured should bring the attendant through from whatever else was so important.

Another minute later, however, he realized that he was on his own. He looked at the bell and considered ringing it again, although he quickly figured that there was no point. Some more white flakes lay on the counter just a little further along, and Wade told himself that the whole motel seemed as if it could use a proper clean.

"Great," he sighed, walking back to the machine and inspecting the offerings again. "What kind of -"

Before he could finish, the lights in the machine flickered, accompanied by a faint buzzing sound. He took a step back, just as the lights behind the counter flickered as well. This flickering continued for a few more seconds before ending, leaving Wade standing all alone in the foyer as he began to wonder just how one motel could be so rundown and sloppy.

"Fine," he said, slipping some coins into a slot on the front of the machine, then tapping at some buttons. "Next time think ahead a little better, Wade."

He waited as the bottles dropped into the

dispenser below, and then he pulled them out. Once he was done, he looked into the machine again, and this time he spotted his own reflection in the glass. Freezing for a second, he saw the guilt in his own eyes and he wondered how he could continued to lie to Lisa.

"You just have to get through this one last time," he told himself, speaking the words out loud in an attempt to make them sink in properly. "You're not a bad person. Well, you probably are, but you're doing it for good reasons. Just think of the baby and..."

His voice trailed off as he felt a tugging sensation in his chest.

"You don't love Lisa," he added. "You never did. You might have thought you did, you might have convinced yourself, but that was just because you're a good actor. It was a game, and a role you were playing, and you never had any actual feelings for her. The entire relationship was fake and Lisa never meant anything to you. You were just..."

He paused, and then he leaned forward and bumped his forehead gently against the front of the vending machine.

"Just get through this and don't do anything stupid," he whispered. "Please, for the love of God, don't do anything you're going to regret. Keep it in your pants, don't get tempted, and don't trick yourself into thinking that you care. Because you don't. You never did." He took a long, slow and very deep breath. "You've got this."

After swallowing hard, he stepped back and headed to the door, carrying the bottles of soda he'd managed to get from the machine. Once he gone the foyer fell still and silent, although the lights flickered again after a few seconds. At the same time, a shadowy figure briefly emerged from around one of the corners, casting a long shadow across the floor. A few seconds after that a toilet flushed in the distance and the shadowy figure pulled back out of sight just as the door behind the counter opened and the attendant wandered out while still buttoning his pants back up.

"Anyone here?" the man asked gruffly. "No? Fine, it can't have been that urgent, then can it?"

He flopped down onto his office chair, which creaked loudly beneath his weight, and then he lifted up his right foot and began to pick at one of the toenails. Muttering to himself, after a few more seconds he leaned down and began to bite the offending piece of nail away, completely unaware that he was being watched by a figure lurking nearby in the shadows.

CHAPTER NINETEEN

Today...

ANOTHER GUST OF WIND blew between the trees, rattling a human skull that sat high up in the branches.

"What *is* this?" John asked, still staring up at the bones with an expression of pure disbelief. "What am I looking at?"

"These are the three missing men from the bus," Susan told him, smiling as she watched the skulls, one of which was more badly damaged than the other two. "I knew they were out here somewhere, I knew they'd be found eventually. One of them must be my dear Timothy, and the other two are the other missing men. They've been here all along."

"How did they get up there?" Tommy asked.

"Good questions," John replied. "They certainly didn't do it themselves."

"And how did they get arranged like this?" Tommy continued. "They're not even in the right shapes." He paused, watching the bones for a moment longer. "Are they symmetrical?"

"They are," John agreed, noting that the various bones had been arranged to form what appeared to be some kind of arch high in the trees. "That's a very deliberate pattern, someone must have put a great deal of thought into all of this. We need to find out who."

"Ask them," Susan said.

John turned to her.

"Don't you hear them?" she continued. "They want to help. They want us to know. When the wind blows through them, they speak and they sing. I used to hear them sometimes even when I was in my bed at home in town, although obviously I didn't know exactly how they were making themselves so loud. And now I see them at last, and they're so beautiful."

"Right," John said cautiously, "but when you said to... ask them..."

"I think they'll answer," she replied. "If you ask nicely, at least. They've been here for so very long, they've been here for four decades, I'm sure they're very much ready by now to tell their story."

"I..."

For a moment, not really knowing how to respond, John could only stare at her. Finally he turned to Tommy, who merely offered an oblivious shrug.

"Timothy," Susan called out, stepping past John and looking up at the three skulls, "I know you're here. I don't know if you recognize me, I'm afraid I'm rather older than I was when you last saw me on our wedding day. I'm all wrinkly and weathered, but I hope you understand that I always stayed loyal to you." She held up one hand to show him the ring she still wore. "I never even took this off. Even though you were taken from me mere hours after our union, I have still been your wife for all these years."

A gust of wind blew a little stronger, whistling through the bones.

"Yes," she continued, "I knew you'd say that, but I never wanted to find anyone else. I love you as much today as I did back then. More, even."

John and Tommy exchanged worried glances.

"I'm just so sorry that you were out here alone like this for so very long," Susan added, still looking up at the bones. "This is what I most feared, in a way. The thought of you lost like this, unable to rest in peace, your body... displayed in such a horrible way. My worst fears have come true, and I just wish I could have found you sooner. I heard your voices, but I couldn't quite make them out properly."

"You need to come with us," John said cautiously, stepping up behind Susan and placing a hand on the side of her arm. "Mrs. Walpole, I have a duty to get you to safety, but as soon as that's done I'm going to send a team out here to examine this site and determine exactly what's going on."

"Why would you do that?" she asked.

"What do -"

"Isn't it obvious?" she continued. "They took Timothy and the two other men and they used them for this... I don't even know what it is, but it's some kind of ritual, isn't it?"

"Let's not jump to conclusions," John replied, as he glanced up at the bones in the trees again. "I really think -"

Before he could finish, he realized that some of the shapes seemed familiar, as if a number of the bones had been arranged in a manner that he'd seen before. For a few seconds he struggled to remember exactly what was causing this sense of familiarity, until finally he remembered the small objects that had been hanging from trees all around Wentworth Stone's mansion.

At that moment, another gust of wind blew through the clearing, rushing through the three skulls and causing a whistling sound to emerge from their mouths. And somehow, in the midst of that whistling sound, John finally heard what seemed to be the faintest hint of a voice.

"Leave," the skulls were saying. "Leave now and forever."

"What *is* this place?" John whispered as a shiver ran through his chest. "What's going on here?"

***

"Goddamn stupid, stubborn, ignorant idiots!"

Stumbling on the rough ground, Joe Hicks almost fell to his knees. At the last moment he reached out and supported himself against a nearby tree, but his ankles and knees were singing with pain and for a few seconds he wondered whether he could go on at all. Taking a series of deep, snatched breaths, he told himself that giving up wasn't an option, that he had to keep going, even if part of him wanted to leave every last one of the ingrates to their fates.

"I'm too old for this," he gasped. "I shouldn't -"

Before he could finish, he spotted something moving ahead, darting low between the trees. He narrowed his gaze a little, but already he was able to make out the shape of a wolf in the distance. After a moment the animal slowed its pace and stopped, turning to look directly at Joe.

"Not today," Joe sneered. "You're being brave, boy, coming this far away from your homeland. You're taking quite a risk."

The wolf merely remained in place, watching Joe carefully as if it was trying to determine whether or not he might be a threat. A moment later a second wolf stepped into view a little further back, followed swiftly by a third.

"Gathering, huh?" Joe said, instinctively reaching for his gun. "I hope you're smarter than that. If there's one thing I've always said about you lot, it's that you're smart. I might not agree with you, but I've never underestimated you."

He kept his eyes on the wolves, fully aware now that he was being judged. In the back of his mind he was already trying to work out whether he'd be able to drop them all; he hadn't expected to face a fight, so he had only the six shots available before reloading, and he knew his aim had been getting worse for some time. In his prime he'd have been supremely confident, able to shoot the three wolves with three bullets left over, but now he wasn't so sure. His hand had developed a tremble and – as much as he hated to admit the fact – he'd been getting just a little sloppy.

But the bullets were silver-tipped, at least. Even a body shot would be enough to drive one of the wolves away. Three, though... he didn't much fancy his chances against three.

"I'll still take at least one of you with me," he whispered as the wolves continued to watch him. "Damn it, see if I don't."

He waited, and a moment later – as if they'd made their decisions at the exact same time – the three wolves turned and began to hurry away through the forest. Joe felt a rush of relief, before glancing over his shoulder to make sure that he wasn't about to be ambushed from behind. Looking ahead again, he saw the wolves disappear into the distance, and he already knew exactly where they were headed. He slowly slipped his gun away, and his mind was racing as he tried to work out what he needed to do next.

"Damn you, John Tench," he muttered finally. "You've been in the job for less than a month, and you're already on the verge of ruining everything I worked to build."

Feeling a growing sense of anger, he set off again, pushing through the forest as fast as he could manage, trying to ignore the pain rippling through his body. All he knew in that moment was that he had to get to the gate before anything bad happened, and that then he'd be able to clear up the mess. That, in a way, had been his job for so many years. He was getting very good at clearing up messes created by other people.

CHAPTER TWENTY

Twenty years earlier...

"SOMETIMES I FEEL LIKE I'm losing my mind," Lisa said as she sat on the end of the bed, staring down at a can of soda in her hands. "Like... I actually think I might be going insane."

"It sounds like you've been through a lot lately," Wade replied, watching her as he leaned against the wall near the bathroom door. "If even half of what you told me is true -"

"If?" she replied pointedly.

"You know what I mean," he told her. "I believe you, Lisa. Thousands wouldn't, but I'm absolutely certain that what you told me happened. I've always trusted you."

"That thing on the road wasn't human," she

replied. "Or at least, it might have been human once, but it was in the process of changing into something else. And then all the stuff with Wentworth Stone and the swans just feels far too bizarre for anyone to take it seriously. Sometimes I think I should charge back out there and demand to see his wife again, but deep down I know that I wouldn't get very far."

"Have you ever considered leaving Sobolton?" he asked.

"Why would I do that?"

"I don't know. Looking for a fresh start, maybe?" He waited for an answer, but he knew deep down that she'd find some excuse to shoot the idea down. "I know it might feel like a big deal," he said after a few more seconds, "but that might be precisely because it's what you need. Lisa, you have a lot of history here and a lot of past. A lot of memories, both good and bad. Have you ever considered the possibility that you could just leave them all behind?"

She thought about the question for a moment, before slowly shaking her head.

"It's a decent idea," he continued. "You've lived here for most of your life and sometimes I think you could use a fresh perspective. You're more than qualified, you could absolutely find a new job in another place. Would moving away really be so bad?"

"I'm Sobolton born and bred," she reminded him. "I wouldn't be able to function anywhere else."

"Are you really functioning here?"

"I can't live anywhere else," she said firmly. "I'm not cut out for making fresh starts."

"You don't know that until you've tried."

"I do," she said firmly, before letting out a heavy sigh. "I can't run away from my problems, Wade. That might be your way of dealing with things, but it's not mine."

"Ouch," he replied drolly.

"I'm not entirely wrong," she added. "The thing is, there's something else. I don't know quite what's happening, but I keep seeing this place in my head. It's a cabin out in the middle of nowhere. I swear I've never seen the place in my entire life, but it keeps popping into my thoughts in such a huge amount of detail. And whenever I see it, I can't shake the sense that it's familiar in some way, that I've definitely been there before."

"Where do you think it is?"

"Somewhere round here."

"And do you really think you've been there?"

She thought about that question for a moment, and then she nodded.

"It's like it's buried in my mind," she explained. "It's like it's a memory that's somehow been squashed deep down in my head, and now it's forcing itself back to the surface. I can't help thinking that it's not alone, either. I know this is going to sound totally insane, but more and more I feel like I've got some kind of hidden or lost memory that's still trapped somewhere in my mind. And now it's trying to break through."

"In what way?"

"I almost feel like it refuses to stay forgotten forever. I feel like I've forgotten how to remember the place, but it's determined to remind me. I know how crazy this all sounds, Wade, but I'm it's like there's this whole set of memories in my head and something's blocking me from accessing them. The worst part is, I don't know whether I've done this to myself or..."

For a few seconds she thought back to the wristband in her desk at the office.

"Lakehurst," she whispered finally.

"Have you spoken to anyone else about this?" he asked.

"I don't trust anyone else," she replied. "Not really. Not the way I trust you. And believe me, it pains me to have to admit something like that." She paused for a few more seconds. "I need to talk to someone who isn't going to instantly think that I need to be locked in a psych ward."

"I'd never think that," he told her.

"You'd be stupid not to."

"I -"

He stopped himself before he could finish.

"Wade," she continued, her voice trembling now with genuine fear, "do you know something that I don't? Do you know something about me? Because if you do, now's the time to tell me."

***

Leaning over the bathroom sink, Wade took a moment to splash cold water on his face. Standing up straight, he looked at his reflection in the cracked and dirty mirror, and he didn't like what he saw staring back: he saw fear in his own eyes, and guilt too, and worst of all he saw uncertainty.

"You have to tread so carefully right now," he whispered, keeping his voice low so that Lisa wouldn't be able to hear him in the bedroom. "Remember, she means nothing to you. You don't love her. It was always just a business arrangement."

Even as those words left his lips, however, he knew that he was fooling himself. He loved Karen, that much was certain, and he wanted nothing more than to go home and wait for their child to arrive. At the same time, in a way that he'd never previously thought possible, he also loved Lisa. As he watched the reflection of his own eyes, he realized that he genuinely loved both women, albeit in different ways; sometimes he wondered whether he was mistaking pity for love, whether he really just felt sorry for Lisa, but deep down he knew that he loved her properly. He knew he had no future with her, not after all the lies he'd told, but he still wanted to try to help her.

"Wade, do you know something that I don't?" he heard her voice asking, echoing through his thoughts. "Do you know something about me? Because if you do, now's the time to tell me."

Swallowing hard, he briefly considered doing just that. He could, he realized, tell her every last damn thing he knew. Sure, she'd be justifiably shocked and furious and heartbroken, but at least she'd know everything and he could leave her with that one powerful gift. At the same time, he felt sure that the truth would break her, that he'd be setting a great burden on her shoulder purely in an attempt to ease his own guilt. He couldn't do that and walk away, and he couldn't risk causing another breakdown in her life.

"Just be strong," he whispered now, even as he felt weaker than ever. "You've done so well to get this far, you just need to get through this conversation and then it's over. Forever."

He took another deep breath.

"You've been a bad person all this time," he added. "For the love of all that's holy, don't ruin it by suddenly trying to be good now. That'd be the worst idea of all. For everyone concerned."

After a few more seconds he felt as if he could at least face her again. Stepping away from the sink, he opened the door and stepped into the bedroom, only to see her already heading for the front door.

"Where are you going?" he asked.

"I can't be here," she replied, pulling the door open and then turning to him. Outside at the far end of the parking lot, traffic was racing past in the early evening gloom as more snow fell. "This was a mistake."

"No, it wasn't," he said, hurrying over to her. "Lisa -"

"I have no right to come here and ask for your help," she told him, cutting him off before he could get another word out. "I'm not your problem, not now."

"Lisa, you were never a problem."

"That's what I feel like," she continued. "I feel like a problem that needs solving, but I've relied for too long on other people to do that solving. There's something wrapped up tight in my head, Wade, and I have to get it untangled. I feel like I've forgotten something, something really important, and I don't know if I can even breathe until I've got it sorted out." Tears were reaching her eyes now and her bottom lip was starting to tremble. "I won't come to you again," she added. "I can't. I need to sort this out on my own, or -"

Suddenly he grabbed her and pulled her closer, kissing her passionately. He pushed her back against the side of the door as the kiss continued, and after a few seconds he felt himself almost involuntarily putting his hands on her waist. In the past, whenever the conversation between them had become awkward, this had been how he'd tried to reset it all; he knew he was making a terrible mistake, and that he was only postponing the pain for both of them, but as the kiss continued he also knew that he couldn't help himself. And as he finally pulled back and looked into her eyes, he knew – with a sense of dread but also relief – that his little tactic was working once again.

Without saying another word, he pulled her to one side and kicked the door shut, and then he pushed her across the room until she fell back onto the bed. He half expected her to resist, or at least for her to try to roll away, but instead she simply stared up at him as he fumbled to get his shirt off. As he fell down on top of her, touching her body as he kissed her again, he knew that he was merely postponing the inevitable, but he also wondered for the first time whether she knew just as well that what they were doing was a terrible mistake.

CHAPTER TWENTY-ONE

Today...

"YOU HEAR THEM, SHERIFF Tench," Susan said, as she and Tommy watched John stepped forward across the clearing. "I know you do. You hear them now."

John opened his mouth to tell her that she was wrong, but – as the wind picked up and the whistling sound emerged once again from the skulls – he couldn't deny that he was hearing occasional words that seemed somehow to be racing down toward him through the snow-filled air.

"You shouldn't be here," the wind whispered. "You're already far too close."

"Take her away," another gust added, with a little more urgency. "I wasn't trying to bring her here. I was trying to warn her to stay back."

"What do you mean, Timothy?" Susan called out. "All I want to do is take you home and give you a proper burial!"

"Microphones," John said under his breath, before hurrying to one of the trees and starting to search for some kind of technical trickery. "Someone has to be using microphones and speakers to do this."

"He doesn't understand," Susan told the skulls. "He seems to have a very closed mind. He's not a local, not like the rest of us."

"Tommy, get over here!" John barked. "I don't know how or why, not yet, but someone has gone to a great deal of trouble to set this whole thing up and I'm going to get to the bottom of it." He headed over to another tree, then another, all the while edging closer to the trees holding the skulls and bones. "Tommy, I'm ordering you to help me find the equipment. I'm not going to be made to look like a fool just so someone can make some kind of point."

"Sheriff," Susan said, watching him with a growing sense of concern, "I think you should be careful."

"Thank you, Mrs. Walpole," he replied, stepping over to another tree and looking up to see the skulls hanging high above, "but I know what I'm doing. Obviously someone is trying to make us look like fools with this primitive nonsense, but we're not going to lower ourselves to their level." He stepped past the tree. "I didn't come all the way to Sobolton just to -"

"John, stop!" a voice boomed suddenly, ringing out from the other side of the clearing.

Stopping in his tracks, John turned to see that Joe Hicks was stumbling into view from the depths of the forest.

"Don't move!" Joe hissed. "I'm being serious now, John. Don't move a muscle!"

"What are you talking about?" John asked.

Pushing past Tommy and Susan, Joe made his way over until he'd almost reached John, and then he looked down at the forest floor. John's left foot had strayed past the line between two of the trees, and Joe hesitated for a moment as if his mind was racing to comprehend what had happened.

"What are you doing here?" John continued. "Joe, have you got anything to do with this nonsense?"

"It's not much," Joe muttered under his breath. "It's half a foot at most." He paused, before reaching out and taking hold of John's hand. "Just step back really slowly. Don't make any sudden movements. If you're really lucky, they won't have noticed."

"Won't have noticed what?" John asked. "Who are you talking about?"

"Will you do what you're told?" Joe sneered, pulling on John's hand. "You've stepped through the gate, but only very slightly. I'm not sure, but I think that means there's still a chance that it's gone unnoticed." He glanced up at the skulls high above. "By most, at least. But if we're lucky, I don't think they'll tell your secret."

"What secret?" John asked, before taking a step back to join Joe. "I don't have a secret."

"Every man has secrets," Joe told him, "but I was specifically talking about what you just did. You might not have realized it, John, but you very nearly stepped through the gate, and if you'd done that... I just hope that I got to you just in time. Your whole foot wasn't through, so hopefully they didn't notice. Even if they did, there might be some kind of loophole that means it doesn't matter."

"Joe, you're not making any sense," John said firmly. "What gate are you talking about? Who are you talking about?"

"They're here," Joe replied, looking past him, watching the forest with a growing sense of fear. "I knew they were. I saw them earlier, but I still don't know that they saw what you did."

"Are you alright in the head?" John asked, before turning to look out into the forest. "I don't -"

Before he could finish, he spotted a wolf in the distance, padding slowly into view. A moment later two other wolves did the same, moving calmly as they kept their eyes fixed on the clearing.

"Given that there aren't supposed to be wolves in the local area," John said cautiously, as he began to reach for his gun, "I sure do keep bumping into the damn things."

"Don't do that," Joe said, grabbing John's hand to keep it away from the gun. "You'll only make them mad."

"I don't care about making them mad," John replied. "I just want to keep them away."

"Do you think they're *trying* to get involved?" Joe asked. "They're only here in the first place because they sensed a disturbance. They're probably just guards, sent here to watch the gate because so many damn stupid humans are getting close. If we back away slowly and carefully, and if we don't give them any reason to worry, I'm pretty sure they'll leave us alone."

"Leave this place," the skulls whispered as another gust of wind blew into the clearing. "Let us make the peace once you're gone."

"Who the hell is doing that?" John muttered, once again looking around for some hint of trickery."

"They're staying calm," Joe continued, pulling John a little further back from the trees. "That's good, it means they probably don't know that you began to step through the gate. With a little patience and discipline, we can massage out any problems here. Let's just keep moving back, and let's make sure that nobody makes any sudden movements that might spook them."

"I'm not going anywhere," John replied, pulling away and turning to him, "until I know exactly what's going on here."

"John, this isn't the time for -"

"I'm the sheriff here and I demand to know what I'm dealing with!"

"Well, maybe you're not the sheriff!" Joe snapped. "Some local idiots might have given you the job, but in the eyes of most people in Sobolton, I'm still the one in charge!" He turned to Tommy. "You understand that, right?" he continued. "Tommy, I'm temporarily relieving Mr. Tench of command and taking control again, and you know that's the best thing for everyone!"

"I'm afraid it doesn't work like that, Joe," John pointed out.

"It works how I say it works!" Joe sneered. "Tommy, you know my authority goes unchallenged round these parts, don't you? You also know that I'm the only one who can keep the peace in this situation. You wouldn't actually want to let this outsider idiot take charge and run things into the ground, would you?" He paused, waiting for a reply, before stepping closer to Tommy. "I'm the sheriff!" he screamed angrily. "You will respect my authority! I'm in charge here!"

Tommy opened his mouth to reply, and then he hesitated for a moment, looking first at John and then back at Joe. For a few seconds he seemed genuinely lost and confused, before finally he stepped across the clearing and took his place firmly next to John.

"I always knew you were another idiot," Joe growled. "You'll regret this choice one day, Tommy."

"What are we going to do, Sheriff Tench?" Tommy asked, keeping his eyes firmly fixed on Joe. "You're the boss. Your word's the law."

"Morons," Joe sneered, shaking his head. "That's the problem with people in this town. You're all just a bunch of sheep, aren't you? You do whatever you're told without even thinking for yourselves. I don't even know why I bother trying to save you. I should have let you all screw things up a long time ago."

"What's really going on here, Joe?" John asked, stepping toward him. "You might be my predecessor, but that doesn't mean I can't haul you back to the station and question you. If I think for one moment that you're involved in any kind of criminal activity, or that you're withholding any information that might be relevant to a case that I'm investigating, I'll throw the book at you until you tell me the truth. So are you going to tell me what's going on now, or do I have to drag you kicking and screaming to the station?"

"You think you're so tough," Joe replied, struggling a little to catch his breath. "Fine, I'll tell you exactly what happened here all those years ago. But trust me, once you know... you'll wish I'd kept it to myself. Because the truth is so much worse than any lie."

CHAPTER TWENTY-TWO

1984...

"MARRIED," SUSAN WALPOLE SAID, staring down with a sense of wonder at the ring on her finger. "You know, I'm really not sure what I expected. I feel different, but I'm not quite sure how."

"I know what you mean," Timothy said, stopping in front of her as some of the other newly married couples made their way toward the bus. "I just keep reminding myself that we've got the rest of our lives to figure it out." He paused, watching her eyes, before allowing himself a grin. "Are you going to be okay for the journey home, Mrs. Walpole?"

"I'm not sure I'll *ever* get used to being

called that," she admitted.

"You will," he said, kissing her on the forehead before taking a step back. "Listen, this idea of the grooms all heading back together might seem stupid, but Mike wants us to put on this big show of making our entrance when we get to town. He thinks it'll cheer everyone up. Let's just humor him and then we've got all evening to celebrate." He paused again, watching her as if he couldn't quite believe that the wedding had finally taken place. "And the rest of our lives," he added. "I love you, Mrs. Walpole."

"I love you too," she replied, before hearing some of the other girls calling out to her. "I'd better go, but I can't wait to just be done with all this unnecessary theater and get on with things. Part of me still wishes that we'd just had a normal wedding. Just the two of us and our families, instead of this... circus."

"What do you think?" Timothy asked, holding up his hand to show her the ring she'd slipped onto his finger earlier. "Some of the other guys were ribbing me about it, but I don't care. I think it looks great. I really want to wear a symbol of our union, Susan, and I don't care if other people think it looks foolish."

"It's beautiful," she told him. "Thank you for wearing it."

"See you in town, Mrs. Walpole," he

laughed as she walked away. "As long as this bus gets fixed, at least."

"Mrs. Walpole," she whispered under her breath, unable to stifle a grin as she hurried over to join the other brides. "I think I'm starting to like the sound of that."

***

"It was a beautiful ceremony," Alison Carter told Susan a short while later, as they stood outside the town hall in the center of Sobolton. "People are going to be talking about this day for years to come. What other town could ever boast having ten weddings on one day?"

"I'm just looking forward to getting on with our lives together," Susan told her, glancing briefly at the road in the hope that the bus carrying the men might arrive at any moment. "Is that boring? I just want to go home with Tim, shut the door to keep the rest of the world out, and have some alone time with him."

"That sounds eminently healthy," Alison replied. "He's such a good man. I'm sure he's going to be the most wonderful husband."

Spotting a familiar figure nearby, Susan felt a flicker of sadness in her heart as Robert Law made his way past.

"Excuse me," she stammered, hurrying

away from Alison and intercepting Robert before he could get to the steps at the front of the town hall. "Bobby, I didn't know you were going to be here today."

"I heard there was going to be a buffet," Robert replied with a smile. "You know me, Susan, I could never resist a buffet, especially if it's free. You look absolutely beautiful, by the way. Timothy's a very lucky man."

"I'm the lucky one," she insisted, before pausing for a moment. "Bobby, I hope things aren't going to be awkward between us. I know things didn't really work out, but I still value you very much as a friend."

"Right back at you," he replied. "You know what? Your father might have had a point, I was very much coasting through medical school, doing the bare minimum I needed to stay on the course. This has been something of a kick up the backside and I'm really applying myself now."

"I'll believe that when I see it."

"Then just wait," he continued. "This time next year, I should have finished my training and then I'll have to decide what I really want to do with my life. I could travel, or I could stick around here in Sobolton. The world's going to be my oyster."

"I know you'll do great things," Susan replied, before reaching out and taking hold of his hands. "And you'll make some lucky lady very

DEAD WIDOW ROAD

happy one day." She hesitated, and then – unable to help herself – she leaned closer and gave him a big hug. "We can remain friends, Bobby, can't we?"

"Of course," he told her. "Just one thing... I'm trying to ditch the name Bobby, just to make myself feel more professional. Can we try Robert?"

"Looking friendly there," a voice chuckled, and Robert and Susan pulled apart just in time to see Deputy Joe Hicks making his way past with a leery grin. "I wouldn't let your new husband see you hugging another man, Susie. Certainly not on your wedding day. Save that for six months from now, when the sheen of fresh love has worn off and you're casting around for a little excitement."

"You little -"

"Don't," Robert said firmly, as Joe made his way into the town hall. "That jumped-up little twerp's looking for a reaction from you. Don't give it to him."

"I can't stand Joseph Hicks," Susan muttered darkly. "I've always hated him. The idea of him one day becoming the sheriff round here fills me with dread."

"Oh, he's certainly got the necessary ambition," Robert replied, "but I'm not sure he'd ever make the cut. Do you have any idea just how seriously that man is disliked?"

Hearing raised voices nearby, Susan turned to see that some of the other brides had gathered to

187

talk to one of the event's organizer. She glanced at the road, and this time she couldn't shake a sense of dread as she realized that the bus carrying the ten husbands still hadn't made its way back into town. Checking her watch, she made a quick calculation and realized that even with time for repairs, there should be some sign of the bus by now.

"Bobby," she said cautiously, "I don't like this. I mean... Robert." She turned to him, and now she couldn't hide the fear from her eyes. "Do you think something's wrong?"

***

"Over there!" Wally Hannigan yelled as he climbed out of his car and rushed over to the side of the road. "There's some kind of disturbance!"

"Stay here," Robert told Susan as he opened the door on his side of the vehicle. "I'm sure it's nothing."

"I'm not waiting anywhere," she replied, clambering out the other side as a couple more vehicles pulled up, including a cruiser from the sheriff's department. "I have to see!"

"Susan," Robert said, turning to her, "this might be upsetting."

"He's my husband!"

Hurrying around past the front of the car, Robert made his way over to join the half a dozen men who'd already gathered at the side of the road. Taking care to make sure that he remained steady on his feet, Robert stopped and looked over the edge, staring down the side of Henge Cliff until he spotted the mangled wreckage of the bus far below. Even in that moment, he felt sure that very few if any of the passengers could possibly have survived.

"There were brake problems, weren't there?" one of the other men said. "I thought they were going to fix it, but if they came round that corner and the brakes failed, they'd have had no time to even scrub any speed before..."

"Where are they?" Susan asked, stopping next to Robert and looking down, then letting out a shocked gasp as she stepped back. "No, it's not possible! That can't be them! Please, they must have got out before..."

"Let me see!" Joe yelled, pushing past everyone else and then stopping to look down at the wrecked bus. "Jesus wept," he continued. "What the hell happened here?"

"There might be survivors," Robert said, hurrying toward the top of the path that led down to the spot where the bus had crashed. "Someone grab my bag from the car and come with me! We have to get to them while there's still time!"

"Timothy!" Susan sobbed, before rushing after Robert, desperate to get down to the bottom of the cliff. "We have to help him!"

"What's going on here?" Albert Friese said, as he and a number of other men hurried over to the top of the cliff and looked down. "Is that..."

"There's been an accident," Joe Hicks replied darkly, unable to stop staring at the wreckage as he felt a growing sense of fear in his chest. A moment later, a solitary wolf howled somewhere in the distance, far out in the forest. "And I'm not sure," he added, "that it's quite over just yet."

CHAPTER TWENTY-THREE

"TIMOTHY!" SUSAN SHOUTED DESPERATELY as she hurried toward the wreckage. "Where are you? Timothy, I'm here!"

Reaching the side of the overturned bus, she began to try to find a way to look inside. Most of the windows had been smashed, and the roof of the bus had been badly dented and deformed; as she hurried around to the other side, Susan tried frantically to look inside until finally she saw that Robert had climbed through one of the few remaining windows that afforded any access at all.

"Where is he?" she shouted, looking through the window and watching as Robert made his way over one of the seats. "What -"

Before she could finish, she spotted a figure slumped in one of the closer seats. She tried to focus on the figure, to work out exactly what she was seeing, but several more seconds passed before she realized that a man was sitting with his head entirely cut away, leaving glistening blood in the exposed stump. His head was resting nearby on one of the other seats, next to a large shard of bloodied glass. As she looked back at the man, Susan realized that she recognized the brown suit that Buddy Lurie had been showing off to all his fellow grooms just a few hours earlier.

"This can't be happening," she stammered, peering past the dead man, only to see another figure that had been partially crushed by the twisted metal roof. "Robert, where's Timothy? Have you found him yet? Is he alright?"

Robert let out a series of gasps as he climbed back to the window, and he cut his hands on broken glass as he clambered back through and dropping out onto the muddy ground. Immediately grabbing Susan, he pulled her away and hugged her tight, forcing her to look in a different direction as several officers from the sheriff's department finally joined them at the scene. A little further back, some bystanders had also made their way down from the side of the road.

"What the hell's going on here?" Joe Hicks snapped. "Are there any survivors?"

"Where's Timothy?" Susan sobbed. "Let me see him!"

"He's not there," Robert replied, squeezing her tighter still, determined to keep her from seeing any more of the mangled bodies. "I counted seven. That means three are missing."

"What do you mean?" Susan whimpered. "How could they be missing?"

"I don't entirely know," Robert said, looking over his shoulder and watching as the officers began to peer into the wreckage. After a moment he spotted thick claw marks cut into some of the metal, and a moment later he turned to look out into the forest as he heard the sound of a wolf howling in the distance. "It's going to be okay, Susan," he continued, unable to hide the fear in his voice. "Just stay calm. We're going to find them."

"I'm not sure we want to," Joe muttered, stepping around to the rear of the bus and looking down at the ground, where a thick trail of blood had been left in the mud, stretching away into the forest. "I think something might have taken them."

***

"No!" Timothy gasped, turning and trying to crawl away across the mud, wincing as he felt his broken ribs jostling for position. "Please, don't -"

Suddenly another of the wolves stopped in front of him. Leaning down, the creature snarled in his face, letting thick drops of saliva hang down from its jaw.

Before Timothy had a chance to beg for his life, he heard a gurgling cry of pain coming from somewhere over his shoulder. Turning, he watched with horror as one of the other men was pulled apart by two other wolves; the man's head was tilting back and they were ripping away from the bloodied neck area, letting the last of his blood gush out onto the ground. Timothy could tell that the man was still just about alive, but a moment later he saw one of the wolves biting down hard, cracking the poor bastard's skull.

"Leave us alone," he murmured, trying to find the strength to get to his feet. He'd been on the ground since the wolves had pulled the three of them from the wreckage, and while he'd been dragged through the forest as well, but now he knew that he had to find some way to get up. "Please, just stop this."

The nearest wolf snarled loudly, taking a solitary step forward. Nearby, bones crunched and Timothy knew that if he looked again, he'd see a wolf eating one of his friends. Instead of subjecting himself to that horror, he pulled back until he bumped against the base of a tree, and then he watched as one of the wolves slowly made its way closer.

"Go away!" Timothy hissed, grabbing a broken branch from nearby and using it in a vain attempt to push the wolf back. "Please, I'm begging you, you have to stop this!"

The wolf tried to move closer, but Timothy managed to flash the end of the broken branch against its face. Letting out a pained snarl, the wolf stepped back before raising its head and howling at the sky.

"You're a big bastard, aren't you?" Timothy sneered, partly in an attempt to distract himself from the sight of his two friends getting torn apart by wolves nearby. "It's funny, I didn't know there were wolves anywhere near Sobolton. In fact -"

As soon as he tried to sit up, he felt an unbearable pain ripping up one side of his back. Worried about showing weakness, he waved the branch at the wolf again, hoping against hope that he might force it away.

"In fact," he continued breathlessly, "I was always specifically told that there were no wolves nearby. Now I think about it, I'm starting to realize that everyone was real insistent on that point, almost as if they were determined to make sure we all believed it. Why was that, huh? Why would people want to hide something like that?"

The wolf tried to move closer again, but once more Timothy was able to bash the side of its head with the branch. Clearly annoyed more than injured, the wolf pulled back a short distance, but only so that it could contemplate another way of attacking.

"I know you're not going to give up," Timothy said firmly. "I also know that soon your buddies are gonna decide to join. My only hope is that we're not too far from where the bus crashed, and by now there should be some people out here looking for us, so..."

He paused, before turning to his right, hoping that a search party might be close.

"Help!" he screamed. "I'm over here! Somebody help me!"

Spotting a flash of movement out of the corner of his eye, he turned just as the wolf lunged at him. Before he even knew what he was thinking, Timothy snarled and jabbed at the creature with the broken stick, and this time he got a lucky break; the branch's splintered tip sliced straight into the wolf's left eye, cutting through and bringing a yelp of pain from the creature's jaw.

Pulling back, with wooden splinters embedded in its bloodied and burst eyeball, the wolf cried out again, this time with enough ferocity to attract the attention of its two companions. Sure enough, the other wolves abandoned their feasts and left the other corpses, making their way over to take a closer look at Timothy.

"Help!" Timothy shouted at the top of this voice, although this time he wasn't brave enough to look away from the wolves, not even for a moment.

"Over here! Please, for the love of God, won't somebody help me?" As tears began to run down his face, he looked at each of the three wolves in turn, and deep down he already knew that he couldn't possibly fight them all off at once.

The wolf with the bloodied eye edged ahead of the other two, snarling louder than ever as if it was ready to take revenge for being partially blinded.

"I won't make this easy for you," Timothy said, adjusting his grip on the branch. "You think I'm gonna be easy pickings? This is one meal that's gonna fight back."

The injured wolf moved closer, but at the last second it suddenly pulled back. At the same time, the other two did the same, as if all three were suddenly scared by something. Timothy held the branch up, convinced that this had to be part of some kind of trick, but a moment later he realized that the wolves seemed to be fearful of something behind him; sure enough, after a fraction of a second he heard a cracking sound, followed by the unmistakable rustling of footsteps moving closer.

"Hello?" Timothy gasped, pushing against the pain and forcing himself to turn around, just in time to see two bare feet stopping just inches away.

He looked up, hoping to see someone from the town, but instead he found himself staring into a pair of dark, unfamiliar eyes.

"What?" he stammered, as the wolves whimpered and backed further away. "I don't... what... who are you?"

***

After stumbling through the forest for a while, Joe Hicks stopped for a moment and looked all around. His eyes darted from one gap to the next, searching for even the slightest hint of movement.

Looking down at the ground again, he realized that the trail had run dry and that there was no more blood mixed into the mud. He set off again as he heard more voices calling out in the distance, but already he was starting to think that they were looking for three needles in one hell of a massive haystack. He knew that the three missing men could have been taken anywhere, and that the odds of finding them – either alive or dead – were astronomically low. As he reached the edge of another clearing, however, he stopped again as he realized that he could hear a voice somewhere nearby.

"Please don't do this," a man was gasping. "Please, I'm begging you, just -"

Suddenly the voice was replaced by an agonized cry, accompanied by the sound of meat getting torn away from bone. Joe instinctively knew that he should turn and run, yet he remained in place as he heard the cries petering out to nothing. In that moment, Joe understood that he'd inadvertently stumbled onto something he should avoid, and a fraction of a second later he spotted a figure standing a little further off, framed in the space between two trees.

"I'm not here," Joe stammered, turning and starting to hurry away. "I'm definitely not here. Please, I don't want to see. I don't want to know. Just pretend I was never here at all."

CHAPTER TWENTY-FOUR

Today...

"EVERY TECHNICAL ANALYSIS OF the bus wreckage said the same thing," Joe continued darkly. "The original accident was just that. An accident. Once the bus had left the road, however, it was fair game. The wolves must have been in the area already, because they were on the scene much faster than any of us could get there. Seven of the people onboard were dead already, but three..."

His voice trailed off for a moment, as a fresh gust of wind blew across the clearing, rattling the bones in the trees.

"Three of the poor bastards weren't so lucky," he explained. "They were dragged away, and their fates were never made public. In truth, quite a long time passed before we really had much idea of what had happened to them, and by then there was no real appetite for the idea of upsetting people. Once I became sheriff, I realized immediately what needed to be done, so I made sure that it was all kept on the down-low. And you might not want to believe me, but to this day I don't think I made the wrong decision."

"What *exactly* happened?" John asked, looking up once again at the bones. "Is this some kind of... ritual?"

"It looks like some kind of demon worshiping set-up to me," Tommy suggested, his voice trembling with fear. "Sir, it's getting darker by the minute. I don't think we should be out here too much longer."

"There are no demons out here," Joe said, keeping his eyes fixed on John. "Demons might be easier to control, in a way. What we're dealing with is something else entirely. It's something that we should really just leave well enough alone." He sighed. "I should know. I once stumbled upon something I had no business being around, and when I tried to run, I very swiftly found out that running doesn't get you very far, not when there's nowhere to hide."

"What exactly are you trying to get at?" John asked.

"Don't try to get me to explain," Joe said

firmly. "John, have you not learned a single goddamn thing from any of this yet? The truth won't help! Hell, the truth might actually make things worse! Just do what I always did, leave the gate alone and pretend it doesn't exist!"

"What gate?" John asked, before looking at the bones again and realizing that they'd been arranged to form a crude by symmetrical arch, stretching the distance between two particularly tall trees. He looked between those trees, and somehow the forest further off seemed darker. "Wait, I think I see it now," he continued. "This thing *does* look like a gate, it's -"

"Stop it, John."

"But why? Where does it lead?"

"Stop it, John," Joe said again, with more venom in his voice now. "I'm ordering you, and begging you at the same time, to stop digging into all of this. We can walk away and leave it behind us, and never think of it again, and hopefully that'll be the end of the matter. There's really no need to start questioning everything and trying to understand it all. Sometimes ignorance is absolutely bliss."

"Someone took the bodies of those three dead men," John said, his mind spinning as he stepped closer to the gate, "and used them to construct this. But why? What's the purpose?"

"You're insufferable," Joe replied, rolling his eyes. "Did anyone ever tell you that? You're completely insufferable."

"The bus crash was forty years ago," John continued, stopping in front of one of the trees, reaching out to touch the trunk. "This seems to have been fairly carefully maintained, as if it's important to someone. What if -"

Before he could finish, he spotted movement ahead. A wolf was slinking through the darkness, followed quickly two more. John instinctively reached for his gun, pulling it from its holster even though he desperately hoped that it wouldn't be needed; keeping his eyes fixed on the wolves, he realized that for now they were clearly keeping their distance, and he noticed after a moment that one of them had a scarred wound covering some kind of old injury to its left eye.

"I think we've established now," John said cautiously, "that there most certainly *are* wolves in this part of the country."

"John, I need you to step back from the gate," Joe replied. "You might not like me and I might not like you, but in this case we're very much on the same side. They really don't take kindly to anyone crossing that threshold without strict permission. The gate has existed for a long time, those bones were only put up there relatively recently as a kind of warning. You already had one near miss, and we really can't afford to have another."

"Stop talking in riddles!" John said, watching the wolves carefully as they divided into two groups. One wolf began to circle the clearing in one direction, with the other two going the opposite way. He wanted to turn and look at Joe, yet at the same time he didn't dare turn his back to such dangerous wild animals. "Who did this to these people all those years ago? Who put the skulls up in the trees!"

"I -"

"And don't try to tell me it was the wolves," he continued. "Don't try to lie to me about that, Joe."

"There are things in this forest that men aren't capable of understanding," Joe told him. "You seem like a smart man, John. You must realize that you've seen some of the shapes before. Look again at the shapes of some of the bones up there, and how they've been arranged. You must -"

"Wentworth Stone," John replied, cutting him off. "I saw similar symbols on Wentworth Stone's estate."

"Bingo," Joe said calmly. "The last person who came blundering into all of this was Stone himself. He caught glimpses of what's out here in the forest and he tried to apply it to his own life. He was meddling with something far greater than he could possibly have imagined, but he thought all his money and learning would keep him safe. I reckon he tapped into about one percent of a percent of the power, and he used it completely wrong, and it still turned his life inside out. By the end he was a rambling old idiot, keeping his dead wife alive by sticking parts of her into swans to keep her going. The crazy part is that his plan almost worked for a while, but no human can master that sort of thing, not in the long run. His life descended into a complete mess of idiotic decisions that, quite frankly, no-one should even be expected to believe. But he stands as a warning, John. Mess with the powers in this forest, particularly with what's on the other side of this gate, and your life might even end up in a worse way than Wentworth Stone's."

"You really believe this stuff, don't you?" John replied, stepping forward. "This gate -"

"This gate has existed for a long time," Joe said, cutting him off. "Forty years ago, a few... decorations were added to make it a little clearer." He stepped over to one of the trees and moved around behind it. "You can go around the gate, and that's fine," he explained, before stepping back past the tree, "but don't ever go *through* it, because that's when you're crossing a boundary you really don't want to cross. That's when they get angry."

"Who?" John asked, even though he couldn't quite believe that he was taking such claims seriously.

"The people who built the gate."

"And who are they?"

As he waited for an answer, John saw that the three wolves were still circling the clearing. The wolf with the scarred eye seemed a little braver than the others, daring to move slightly closer as it let out a snarling growl. Something was clearly holding the wolves back, but John knew that they might yet attack.

"Here's what's going to happen," Joe said firmly. "You're gonna take Mrs. Walpole home and tuck her up in bed, and... I don't know, get her tied down or something so she doesn't come out here again. And then you're going to forget that any of this happened, just like I always tried to pretend that I didn't know what was out here. That way, everyone's happy and no-one has to get hurt."

"Sir," Tommy said cautiously, "my head -"

"Shut up, Tommy," Joe snapped angrily. "I'll talk to you later on the subject of loyalty."

"You need to listen to him," Tommy added, turning to John. "This man knows the truth, and the consequences of crossing the boundary uninvited will be severe."

"Not you too," John sighed. "Tommy -"

"That's not Tommy," Joe said, watching Tommy with a growing sense of concern. "I've seen this before, John. It's even happened to me once or twice. You've really gone and screwed things up. You've gone and got their attention, and that's never a good thing."

"What are you talking about?" John asked, turning to him and then looking back at Tommy. "I swear, sometimes I think this whole town has lost its mind."

"Do not cross the boundary," Tommy said firmly, fixing him with a determined glare. "Anyone who crosses the boundaries will be punished. That is how it has always been, and it's how it always *will* be. We will defend our land. If necessary, to the death."

"Leave," the skulls groaned as wind blew through the gate. "Leave now before it's too late."

CHAPTER TWENTY-FIVE

Twenty years earlier...

OPENING HER EYES, LISA saw the red numbers on the front of the alarm clock and realized that she must have fallen asleep. She blinked a couple of times, convinced that she'd been dreaming but unable to remember any of the details, and then she turned to see Wade sleeping on the other side of the bed.

"Damn it," she mouthed silently, as she realized that she'd done the one thing she'd sworn not to do on her way to the motel.

For a moment, it all came flooding back. She felt as if she and Wade had both been willing to do whatever it took to avoid talking, as if they'd both known that talking would be a bad idea; sex had been a way to avoid getting too intimate, to keep from opening up in any way that might cause lasting damage. At least sex was simple and easy, it was something that everyone understood and a language that needed no translation. Words, on the other hand, could get so complicated so fast.

Words were far more dangerous than sex.

Sitting up, she began to make a plan. Her clothes were scattered across the floor, so she climbed carefully out of the bed and began to gather everything up, slipping items on as soon as she found them. She continually glanced back at the bed, horrified by the idea of waking Wade, but soon she was fully dressed and – as she picked up her shoes – she figured that she could finish outside. Stepping over to the door, she fumbled for a moment with the latch, muttering a few angry curses under her breath as she tried to get away. For some reason the latch wasn't cooperating, almost as if it was conspiring to stop her crossing the threshold and getting out of the room.

"Are you leaving?"

She froze, and in that moment she knew that she hadn't quite been successful. She turned and saw that Wade was sitting up in the bed. The stupid obstinate no-good downright lousy latch had won.

"I thought it would be better," she said cautiously. "I just thought... I didn't see the need for some kind of long conversation. I just... I wasn't being rude, I really just thought it'd be the best thing."

"Yeah," he murmured, running a hand through his hair. "Lisa, I swear I wasn't planning this."

"Me neither," she said quickly.

"In fact," he continued, "I swore it wouldn't happen. You have to believe me."

"I believe you," she told him, keen to get the conversation over before it could progress to become anything more substantial. "Let's just pretend it didn't happen at all. Let's just not see or contact each other again, okay? We're over, Wade, and obviously it's bad news whenever we meet again."

"We seem to have this connection," he suggested.

"I wouldn't use that word," she muttered.

"I would," he told her. "Then again, I don't suppose it matters, not now. The important thing is, I never meant to hurt you."

"I don't care," she replied, turning and fumbling with the latch once again. "What's wrong with this thing? Why won't it open?"

"It's temperamental," he explained. "You have to jiggle it up a little and then to the left."

"That's not working."

"Try pushing a little harder."

"It's still not working!" she hissed, annoyed now by her inability to master something as simple as opening a door.

"Just try pushing."

"I know how to push!" she snapped angrily.

"Let me help," he muttered, grabbing some clothes and quickly getting dressed, then heading over.

"I can do it," she told him.

"Just jiggle it up and -"

"I heard you the first time," she said firmly, pushing harder and harder on the latch, determined to get it open without any assistance. "I'm not an idiot, Wade. I've opened doors before."

"Now you're just -"

"Can you just leave me alone?" she hissed. "It's almost budging, I just need to -"

Before she could finish, the entire latch broke away from the door, falling into her hands and then dropping in several pieces to the floor. All that was left on the door now was a set of holes where the screws had gone, and a few parts of the lock poking out uselessly.

"Now you broke it," Wade pointed out.

"I know," she said through gritted teeth. "I can see that for myself."

"You had to jiggle it and -"

"It you say that one more time, I'll kill you," she replied, before sighing again as she realized that she was letting him get to her. "I'm sorry, I must have pushed too hard in the wrong direction. I'll pay for the damage."

"It was going to come off anyway," he said, grabbing what remained of the lock as Lisa stepped aside. He took a moment to fiddle with the various pieces before managing to get the door open. "There. It's easy when you know how, but I admit it takes a while to get the hang of it." He waited for a reply, and after a moment a faint smile spread across his lips. "I've got a lot of experience with crappy motel rooms," he added. "They all have their idiosyncrasies, you kinda have to learn to live with them. The key is to just not get annoyed and to try to stay logical."

"Thanks," she murmured, barely able to make eye contact with him as she slipped past and stepped outside into the cool night air.

"I guess this is goodbye, then," he said.

She muttered something else, something that he didn't even hear properly, as she headed toward her car.

"I'm sorry for hurting you, Lisa," he called after her. "Even tonight, I never meant to cave so easily. I hope you know that I truly loved you."

Reaching her car, she stopped and looked back at him.

"Things just didn't work out," he continued, wishing he could tell her the whole truth while knowing full well that he could never be that cruel. "No matter what I did, I want you to understand that my feelings for you were genuine. I'd hate to feel like you doubted me or... like you thought I was lying all the time." He waited, and then he watched as she simply climbed into the car and drove away. "I'm sorry, Lisa," he added under his breath, watching as her car disappeared into the distance. "God speed. I hope you find whatever it is that you're looking for."

***

"You're an idiot," Lisa said through gritted teeth, struggling to see the road properly as tears filled her eyes. "When are you going to stop being so stupid? When are you going to stop taking the easy way out all the damn time?"

Wiping her eyes, she saw that the lights

ahead were red now. As she brought her car to a stop at the junction, she took a deep breath and told herself that she just needed to crawl into her own bed and – preferably – never crawl out again. More than anything, she wanted to rewind the previous few hours and find some way to stop herself falling for Wade's charm again; she felt as if he'd wrapped her around his little finger and played her for a fool, but deep down she knew it was all her fault. On her way over to the motel, telling herself that she only needed to talk, hadn't she known in some way that they'd end up doing more than just talking?

After all, Wade had always found a way past her defenses. The sentries of her heart had a tendency to set down their weapons whenever he was near.

"Come on," she muttered, wondering why the light was taking so long to turn green. She wasn't even far from home now, and as she glanced at the dashboard she saw that 9pm would be rolling around soon. Drumming her fingers on the wheel, she felt an overwhelming urge to get away from the world.

In that moment, she wanted nothing more than to simply disappear.

Finally the light turned green. Relieved, Lisa put the car in gear and began to drive again, making her way along the road that would eventually lead her all the way to her apartment. Fresh tears were filling her eyes, tears of sorrow but also tears of anger, and she supposed that -

Suddenly a shape rushed out in front of the car, and Lisa slammed her foot on the brakes so hard that she was jolted forward as the vehicle came to a halt.

Staring out through the windshield, Lisa saw some kind of animal standing in front of the car, staring at her though the falling snow. She blinked a couple of times, and after a few seconds she realized to her astonishment that she was staring at a beautiful, fully-grown gray wolf. No matter how hard she tried to tell herself that this was impossible, that there weren't supposed to be any wolves at all in the Sobolton area and that they certainly wouldn't enter the town itself, she couldn't help but look into the animal's eyes. Opening her mouth to call out, she realized at the last moment that she had nothing to say, and she was struck instead by the vast intelligence that seemed to be watching her from behind the wolf's eyes.

And the sickness.

After a moment she realized that the wolf was very thin, almost dangerously so, and that it appeared to have some kind of mange on one side of its body. This was clearly an animal struggling to feed itself, which perhaps wasn't surprising if it was reduced to foraging in the town. Sometimes the edges of the town and the forest became blurred and animals from either side were prone to straying in the wrong direction. Now, bathed in the traffic lights and the beam from the car, the wolf looked utterly out of place, as if it was strung out on the limbs of death.

For a few seconds, stretching out to last an eternity, Lisa and the wolf simply stared at one another. Then, as if spooked by some distant noise, the wolf turned and hurried away, racing through the snow and picking up speed as it ran behind the diner.

"Okay," Lisa said, still struggling to come to terms with what she'd just seen. "That was... intense."

Suddenly a car horn blared, and she saw another vehicle in her mirrors. Realizing that she was blocking the road, she muttered a few apologies under her breath before setting off again, driving through the town on her way home. Ahead, beyond the limits of Sobolton, the dark forest spread out for miles and miles.

CHAPTER TWENTY-SIX

Today...

"BABY, YOU'RE THE ONE I need, the one I've always needed. When I think of you with that other guy, my hearts starts pounding and bleeding. You're the light of my -"

Stopping suddenly, still sitting on a ledge at the bottom of Henge Cliff, Doctor Robert Law furrowed his brow.

"These are the worst lyrics in the world," he added after a moment. "It's fine when you're singing along in the car, but when you just sing them by yourself a cappella like this... I mean, I'm no poet, but I'm pretty sure I could do better. Damn it, maybe I *should* have started that band when I was young after all."

Hearing a rustling sound, he turned to see that several of the officers were making their way back from the depths of the forest. Immediately getting to his feet, he waited for some sign of John and Susan, but after a few seconds he realized that they were nowhere to be seen.

"What's going on?" he asked. "Did you find her?"

"Is Sheriff Tench here?" Billy Sutter asked.

"No, Sheriff Tench isn't here," Robert said cautiously. "Neither's Tommy. I thought they were with you."

"I don't mind admitting, we sorta got a little lost of there," Billy continued, removing his hat and wiping his brow. "There was a moment back there where I started to worry that someone'd need to send out a search party for *us*."

"Where are the others?" Robert asked, unable to hide a sense of frustration.

"I'm sure they'll be back soon," Billy told him. "I hate to say this, but I think maybe it's getting a little too dark for the search to continue. It might be better if we shut things down for the rest of the day and wait until morning. The terrain's really tough and the conditions are getting worse. We can't continue the search right now."

"And leave an elderly woman walking around in this weather, lost and alone?" Robert replied incredulously. "Are you serious? She'd never last the night!" He hesitated for a moment, before leaning on his stick as he began to make his way toward the trees. "You might be willing to call it a night, but I refuse to stop until we've found her. I'll just have to go out there myself and -"

Suddenly a gunshot rang out in the distance, echoing through the forest, followed a fraction of a second later by another.

"What was that?" Billy stammered. "What... who's shooting out there?"

***

"Tommy, what are you playing at?" John asked a few minutes earlier, feeling increasingly weary as he realized that everyone seemed determined to mess with him. "Please, I really need you to keep a cool head."

"Incursions across the boundary are not taken lightly," Tommy replied firmly. "Others have made the same mistake, and we have always had to take action, however reluctantly. We cannot make exceptions."

"I have to find Timothy," Susan murmured, stepping past John. "That's all I came out here for."

"Here's what's going to happen," John said firmly. "Tommy, we're taking Mrs. Walpole home, and we'll get Robert Law to check her over. Joe, you're coming to the station so you can answer my questions properly, and I should warn you that I'm not in the mood for more nonsense. I want answers, and I don't want more of this mystical bullshit. Is that clear?"

"People told me you were a straight man," Joe replied. "They told me you were a strong fellow who didn't take crap from anyone. I thought maybe, just maybe, that might work out, but now I see the truth. Did you ever stop to realize, John, that sometimes a man can be *too* straight and strong and good?"

"Now you're doing it again," John sighed. "Joe, I'm rapidly running out of patience and -"

"Susan, stop!" Joe shouted, taking a step forward as he looked past John, then stopping in his tracks. "Susan, what are you doing?"

Turning, John saw that Susan had made her way between the trees, passing beneath the so-called gate and then stopping a little further off toward the darkness. Before he had a chance to react, John saw that the three wolves were gathering a short way ahead, watching Susan closely as the animal with the scarred eye began to make its way closer.

"Get away from her!" John shouted, hurrying to Susan and pulling her back through the gate.

"I just want to find Timothy," she sobbed, looking up at the bones. "I hear his voice, but I hate to think of him trapped up there. His spirit must be close, mustn't it?"

"Now you've done it," Joe snarled. "You stupid old woman, do you have any idea what any of this means? Anyone who steps through the gate without permission has to be punished, that's just about the most basic rule of the whole situation, even a complete idiot should be able to figure it out." He paused for a moment. "That goes for you too, John. Even if it was only for a moment, if you crossed the boundary then -"

"Shut up!" John snapped at him, momentarily losing his cool. "I don't want to hear any more of this crap!"

Shocked by his own anger, he took a deep breath.

"I'm sorry," he added, "I didn't mean to lose my temper like that. It was unprofessional of me and wrong, and I apologize, but the point still stands. We need to stick to the facts in this situation."

"The short fat man is correct," Tommy explained calmly. "Transgressions must be paid for, and the only currency our two worlds share is blood."

"Have you been drinking?" John asked him. "Are you high on something?"

"I've had enough of this," Joe said darkly, pulling a gun from his holster and checking that it was loaded. "I'm taking charge. Call it a mutiny if you want, John, but I'm temporarily re-installing myself as sheriff so that I can clean up this mess that the rest of you have created. Don't even bother to argue with me, because I don't care what you think. I'll find some loophole, some bylaw of a bylaw in some document that authorizes me to do this, and if I can't then I'll just make one up."

He turned and aimed the gun directly at John's face.

"Are you gonna fight me on this?" he continued. "Or are you gonna recognize that this is my right?"

"Put the gun down, Joe," John said firmly.

"You can have the job back eventually," Joe sneered. "Maybe. If I feel like it. But it's clear to me now that I should never have vacated the office. I should have stood up to those idiots who said my time was done, I should've just ignored them and carried on with the job. Well, that's what I'm gonna do from now on. And if you still think you can argue with me, John, then that's too bad. But now that I'm the sheriff again, I'm sure I can come up with a story to explain you taking a shot to the face. Then I'll get on with fixing all the messes you've created."

"Put the gun down, Joe," John said again. "It's a criminal offense to -"

"Don't quote the law at me, my boy," Joe

replied. "The law's whatever I say it is, and it's been that way for as long as I can remember. Even before I was sheriff round here, I called the shots. Who do you think took charge on that day when the bus crashed? Who do you think realized right from the start that there was no point fighting against what had happened? Who do you think stumbled out here and saw what was happening to those three men, and who do you think had the strength and courage to turn his back and accept reality?"

"You need to be telling me this in a room with a tape recorder," John reminded him, "with a lawyer present and -"

"That's your problem!" Joe snapped. "You always think the rules are going to save you, but they're not! It's strength that wins the day, John!" He adjusted his grip on the gun. "It's strength and -"

"Shame on you!"

Suddenly Susan pushed Joe hard, almost knocking him off his feet.. He turned and aimed at her, but she pushed him again, then for a third time, and this time he fell back and landed with a heavy thud on the ground.

"You knew!" she sobbed, standing over him as tears ran down her face. "You knew all along, didn't you? You knew what had happened to my dear Timothy and you never told anyone! All these years, all this fear and uncertainty, and you could have stopped it all if you'd just told the truth."

"Not another one," Joe muttered angrily, wincing as he struggled to get back on his feet. "Do you know what the problem is round these parts? This town's going soft, that's the problem. Seems like I'm gonna have to do a little more tidying up than I'd planned, but that's fine with me." He took a moment to get his breath back, and then he allowed himself a faint smile. "It's not my fault that sometimes I even enjoy my job."

With that, he aimed the gun directly at John's face and fired, and then he aimed at Susan and fired again.

CHAPTER TWENTY-SEVEN

Twenty years earlier...

THE DOOR TO LISA'S bedroom stood wide open as – in the distance – her key turned in the lock of the front door.

As soon as she was inside, Lisa leaned back, pushing the door shut as she took a deep breath. A few seconds later, unable to stop herself, she slid down until she was sitting on the floor. Simultaneously exhausted and wired, she felt as if her mind was racing so fast that she could barely keep track of her thoughts; she couldn't help replaying the evening over and over again, regretting every moment of her passionate encounter with Wade. She'd been so certain that she wasn't going to let him do that to her, so convinced that she'd be able to resist, and yet...

And yet he'd dragged her into bed almost immediately, as if that had been the only way either of them knew how to end a conversation.

Hearing a creaking sound, she looked along the corridor and saw the open doorway leading into the bedroom. She felt absolutely certain that she'd shut that door earlier, yet now it stood wide open and she was once again struck by the fear that someone else might be in the apartment. She'd felt the same suspicions many times now, to the extent that she was almost bored by the fear, yet at the same time she couldn't quite shake the worry that nothing in the apartment was ever quite right.

"Is anyone there?" she called out, not for the first time. "Is anyone..."

Her voice trailed off as she realized that there was no point even trying. How many times had she shouted out the same questions in the same situation, only to end up feeling like a fool? She'd always worked so hard to hold her mind together, to force herself to stay strong, and she hated the idea that a few bumps and creaking noises might undo all of that effort.

"There's no-one there," she added firmly, telling herself that she simply had to convince herself of that fact. "It's fine. I get it now. There never was."

Hauling herself up, she began to look

around the kitchen. At first she saw no sign of anything untoward, but finally she spotted some more of the small white flakes near the stove. She stepped closer and looked at the flakes, and now she was really starting to wonder where they came from; she'd been finding them not only at home but also in the office, and there was really no obvious source. Picking up one particularly large flake, she held it against a light and saw that it was creased and marked, almost like the transparent surface of some asteroid-impacted planet, but also that there were a couple of small holes, almost as if...

Skin.

The white flakes were pieces of skin.

"I'm losing my mind," she whispered, still mesmerized by the flake before carefully setting it down. "I can't keep going like this, I -"

Before she could finish, she suddenly saw the forest in her mind's eye, with the little pinprick of light punctuating the darkness. This was the same sight she'd spotted while she was out at Mike Dingle's farm, and she couldn't shake the feeling that the light was calling her somehow; she told herself that she couldn't possibly know where the light had been coming from, yet somehow she felt fairly sure that she could find the place. No matter how crazy the idea sounded, and no matter how much she tried to tell herself that she shouldn't go back out into the forest at night, she already knew deep down that she wasn't going to be able to resist the lure.

Finally she made her way across the apartment and started gathering all the things she was going to need. She took the rifle and slung it over her shoulder, then she made sure that she had ammunition, and then she made her way to the door. She knew that the answer was out there somewhere, and she knew she couldn't wait a moment longer.

***

Several hours later, having trudged a few miles from the road, Lisa stopped for a moment in the pitch-black forest and looked around. She knew that any rational observer would call her crazy, that she should turn back and go home, yet somehow she felt compelled to keep going, pushing through the darkness as she continued to search for whatever was missing.

Somewhere nearby an owl hooted. Lisa turned and looked between the trees. She knew that the forest would come alive at night, that lots of creatures would have emerged now that the light had faded. The owl hooted again, almost as if offering a warning, but Lisa told herself that she couldn't afford to heed any warnings, not when she felt she was getting closer to some kind of answer. And as she looked around at the trees again, shining her flashlight at their twisted branches, she was struck by one overwhelming thought.

I've been here before.

As she set off again, she told herself that she had to be wrong, that there was no way anyone would be able to recognize some random space in the forest. The sensation persisted, however, and after a few more steps she stopped again as she realized she could hear a faint rattling sound coming from somewhere nearby. She looked around, and as a gentle breeze blew through the forest she heard the wind twisting and howling in her ears, almost forming words.

And the same thought hit her again.

I've been here before.

She'd been to the forest with her father many times, of course, and as she set off again she supposed that he might have taken her out into this particular area. He'd tried to get her into hunting and fishing, although she'd never really enjoyed the idea of killing animals, and eventually he'd accepted the inevitable. As she picked her way past some more trees, she wondered whether she perhaps remembered more of the forest than she'd realized, although that explanation didn't quite sit right. Finally, as her legs began to ache, she heard the rattling sound again, and this time when she looked up she spotted various objects hanging from the trees high above.

"You're not an outdoor kind of girl," she remembered her father telling her many years earlier. "I suppose that's okay, there's no point forcing it. You can't make yourself become someone you're not."

She aimed the flashlight's beam straight up and saw that the objects were swinging slightly in the wind. A few of the strange items looked a little like bones, and after a few more seconds she realized that one of them was a human skull.

"What the..."

As the wind continued, blowing through the bones, Lisa heard the howling sound digging deeper into her ears. She felt as if she was on the verge of hearing some kind of message, but – if so – it was a message that never quite emerged.

"You're so far out of your comfort zone," her father's voice continued. "You should listen harder and pay attention to the warning. Of course, for that to happen you need to stand still for five minutes and actually pay attention to the world that's around you. Can you do that, Lisa?"

Spotting two more skulls, one on either side of the first, Lisa realized that this collection of human bones had been arranged quite carefully, almost as if someone had been trying to create some kind of arch or gateway. She felt a shiver pass through her chest as she realized that these bones reminded her a little of the strange symbols she'd seen up at Wentworth Stone's estate, although she quickly told herself that this was merely a coincidence. After all, Stone's place was several miles away and she felt fairly sure that he wouldn't be involved with anything far out in the forest.

Yet as she continued to stare at the bones, she was once again struck by the thought that had been circulating though her mind for a while now.

I've been here before.

No matter how hard she tried to tell herself that she was wrong, she couldn't shake the sense that somehow – in some way, perhaps a long time ago – she'd definitely seen these particular bones hanging in these particular trees in this particular clearing. The sense of familiarity seemed utterly alien and inexplicable, yet it persisted for several seconds and seemed almost to become stronger.

The bones rattled again, and Lisa looked around to make sure that she was truly alone. She felt more than ever that she should turn and go back to her car, but she also worried that she'd gone too far now to simply give up on her quest. More than ever before, she felt she knew which way to go, that she could find the light that she'd seen burning in the forest, so finally she began to make her way forward.

Stepping between the two tall trees, and passing directly beneath the gate formed by the bones, she set off into the darkness, forcing her way deeper and deeper into the forest.

CHAPTER TWENTY-EIGHT

Today...

"WHAT..."

Unable to believe what had just happened, Joe pulled the trigger again; the gun fired straight at John's face, yet there was no impact and the bullet fell harmlessly spent to the ground.

"What?" Joe snarled, firing yet again, only to find that he was out of ammunition.

"What happened?" Susan gasped, taking a step back.

"Son of a bitch!" Joe snapped, reaching into his pocket for more bullets, then freezing as soon as he looked down at the forest floor. He saw his own feet, and in that moment he realized that he knew what was wrong: he was several steps across the boundary, having been pushed there earlier by Susan. He was trying to shoot between worlds.

"Weapons don't reach through the gate," Tommy said calmly. "Any weapon used on one side will have no effect on the other."

"No, but I didn't..."

Joe's voice trailed off as he continued to look at the forest floor. After a moment he looked up at the gate high above, and a few seconds later he spun around as he heard the rustling sound of wolves edging closer. His mind was racing as he tried to think of some loophole, some way to escape the crushing inevitability that even now he felt starting to fill his soul.

"I didn't mean to!" he stammered. "I was pushed, it's not fair, I only -"

As the wolves edged closer still, Joe's mouth hung open for a few more seconds before finally he let out a faint sigh.

"Come on," he continued, "there has to be another way. It can't be this simple."

The wolves were moving closer, their eyes locked on Joe as if they were preparing to strike.

"I get it," he muttered. "Intent doesn't really matter, does it? You cross the boundary, then you cross the boundary. It's as simple as that." He hesitated, and then he tossed the gun aside. "I'm not gonna fight it. I've always considered myself to be a smart man, but every run has to come to an end eventually. I thought I had more time, but in some ways I guess this feels more appropriate. Damn it, I just..."

As the wolves began to encircle him, tears reached his eyes.

"I was so careful for so long," he continued, before looking over his shoulder, fixing his gaze on John. "You're probably chuckling to yourself," he sneered, "but enjoy it while you can. There are two types of people in this world, Sheriff Tench. There are people who are losers their whole lives, and then there are people who are winners for a while, but they lose eventually. No-one ever wins, not really. Not when the end comes."

"Joe, come back over here," John said, stepping toward him. "Don't let -"

"No," Tommy said, grabbing his arm and holding him back. "Everyone who crosses the boundary uninvited must pay with their life. Some instantly, some a little while later, some later still, but eventually the debt always becomes due. In this case, it must be paid immediately."

"Joe, get away from the wolves!" John called out. "Joe, don't just stand there!"

"You still don't get it, do you?" Joe replied with a heavy sigh. "John, there are no words that can fix this now. You have to respect the rules of this place, and one of the rules is that -"

Suddenly one of the wolves lunged at Joe,

biting him hard on the arm and knocking him down, causing the other two wolves to rush over and start attacking his neck and shoulders. Screaming, Joe tried to push them away, but he was powerless to resist as all three wolves took turns to rip thick chunks of flesh from his body.

"We have to help him!" John shouted.

"We can't," Tommy replied, holding him in place with uncustomary ease, refusing to let him rush forward. "This is his time to pay for his transgression. In his case, there is to be no delay to the punishment. It must, and was always destined to, end this way."

"God damn you!" Joe gurgled, as one of the wolves ripped the side of his throat away and blood began to burst from his mouth. "This is all your fault, John! If you'd listened to me, no-one would have had to get hurt! Now you'll -"

Before he could finish, the wolf with the scarred eye bit the side of Joe's head, twisting its jaw and starting to rip the skin from the man's face. Joe tried again to cry out, desperately attempting to get some words from his bloodied lips, but a moment later the wolf bit down harder; its teeth crunched into Joe's temple and cheek, forcing the eyeball from its socket and sending a cascade of blood gushing out onto the forest floor.

John tried again to break free from Tommy's grip, but he found that he was unable to escape.

Although he was still trying to cry out, Joe was powerless to resist as one of the wolves began to dig into his belly, quickly ripping out his intestines. The three wolves were pulling in different directions now, starting to rip the man's corpse into different pieces, and Joe's final scream came as his left arm was dislocated from his shoulder and torn away, leaving behind stringy lengths of muscle as more and more blood spread across the ground.

"We have to do something!" John shouted, still struggling to break away from Tommy. "How are you doing that?" he asked, looking down at Tommy's hand and trying to loosen his fingers. "Tommy, I don't know how this is working, but you have to let me help him!"

"He's beyond help now," Tommy said calmly, watching as Joe's body was ripped apart before their eyes. "He crossed the boundary without asking permission. He always knew that this would be the result."

"It's horrible," Susan stammered, having covered her eyes with her hands earlier but now daring to look. "I never liked Joe Hicks, but that poor man..."

A shudder ran through her bones.

"No-one should have to die in such a horrible way," she added, before looking up at the bones hanging high above. "Not Joe Hicks, and not anyone else."

The wolves were tugging hard now, ripping Joe's corpse into smaller and smaller pieces, and in some instances pulling chunks of his bloodied flesh out from his clothes. Although he'd stopped actively screaming, Joe was still emitting a series of jagged groans from his mouth, more as a result of air being forced up through his dead throat than down to any kind of persistence; soon even this stopped, as the wolves ferociously ripped his head away from his shoulders, with one of the creatures taking a moment to aggressively throw the severed head across the ground.

"The punishment is complete," Tommy explained. "He was not blind to the risks involved. Of all those gathered here today, he more than the rest should have known that transgression would mean death."

A gust of wind blew through the clearing, rattling the bones high above and bringing a whistling moaning sound from the empty sockets where one they'd had eyes.

"We should have helped him!" John hissed, finally managing to pull away from Tommy's grasp. "We should have... done something! Anything!"

"He was but the first to be punished for tonight's actions," Tommy explained, watching as the wolves began to slink away from the scattered remains of Joe's bloodied corpse. "All shall be punished eventually. Some immediately." He paused, before turning to Susan. "Some soon." He turned to John, staring for a moment. "And others when the time is right. I must warn you, however, that..."

His voice trailed off, and slowly he reached up and put his hands on the sides of his head.

"I must warn you..."

Stepping back, he let out a pained gasp before dropping to his knees. Shaking his head, he seemed to be trying to dislodge something from his ears.

"My head!" he stammered. "Sir, my head really hurts! It's like it's throbbing harder than ever, I swear I can feel my brain almost -"

Before he could get another word out, he leaned forward and vomited across the ground. Struggling to get any air into his lungs, he tried to cry out. A moment later, Doctor Robert Law hurried into view, reaching the clearing and stopping for a moment as he leaned on his walking stick.

"What happened out here?" he gasped breathlessly. "John, is anyone hurt? I heard gunshots!"

"I don't know what happened," John replied, turning to look over at what remained of Joe's corpse. "Not exactly. The gun was pointing right at my face, the bullet fired but..."

His voice trailed off as he recalled the sight

of the fun firing. He told himself that there must have been a simple mistake, that perhaps the gun had been aimed slightly to one side, but deep down he knew that wasn't true. The gun had been shot directly at his face, yet somehow the bullet had seemingly dropped from the air and landed on the forest floor. Then the same thing had happened when Joe had aimed at Susan.

"There's an explanation," he murmured. "There has to be an explanation."

"Susan, are you okay?" Robert asked, hurrying to her just as she began to drop to her knees. "Susan, it's okay, I'm here! Susan, I need you to listen to me! Everything's going to be alright, we're going to get you to an ambulance and then at the hospital we'll patch you up!"

"I found him," she murmured, leaning back in his arms. "I don't know what's wrong, Bobby, I suddenly feel very weak. I think I crossed the line, the same line that Joe crossed. I think..."

"Hold on!" Robert hissed, before looking up at John as Tommy continued to gasp for breath on the ground. "John, do something! Grab her legs! We're going to have to carry her back to the road!"

"I found Timothy," Susan whispered, as tears of joy filled her eyes. Reaching up, she touched the side of Robert's face. "After all these years, I finally found him. Promise me that you'll bury us together. That way... at last, he'll be able to rest in peace. With me. Together, the way we always should have been in life." She ran a hand across his cheek. "I loved you, Bobby. In my own way. And I always knew that... you..."

"Hold on!" Robert said firmly, clearly panicking as Susan's eyes slipped shut. "Damn it, Susan, I can help you if you just hang on until we get to the hospital!" As tears filled his eyes too, he stroked the side of her face. "Susan, can you hear me? It's Bobby, I'm right here. Come on, Susan, you've still got good years ahead of you, there's still so much for you to fight for. Just try to focus on my voice and stay with me. Together we can get you through this."

"My head hurts so much," Tommy gasped, sitting up and looking around, then spotting the mangled parts of Joe's corpse on the other side of the gate. "Wait... what happened here? Where's Joe?"

"I need every man we've got out here," John said firmly, unable to hide a growing sense of anger. "Now!"

"She's gone," Robert said softly, as he gently closed Susan's eyes. "Damn it, she's gone. It's like she just gave up on living." A solitary, long-delayed tear trickled down his cheek. "It's like it was just her time to go."

CHAPTER TWENTY-NINE

Twenty years earlier...

AS DRIVING SNOW FELL harder and faster than ever before, Lisa stopped once more and leaned against a nearby tree tree. Although she'd worn her usual get-up for exploring, this time something was different: freezing water had penetrated her boots and pants, and she was starting to shiver as she realized that she'd lost most of the sensation in her hands.

"Okay," she stammered, her teeth chattering wildly, "this... you might... gone a little too far."

She'd known from the outset that she shouldn't set out into the forest at night, but she'd been driven by an overwhelming determination to get to the truth. Now – worried that she was on the verge of hypothermia – she began to realize that even her thoughts weren't quite making sense, as if her brain was starting to freeze. She looked around, and as she saw trees in every direction she realized that her vision was becoming a little blurry. In that moment she understood that she was more than just cold; she knew now that she was in real danger of freezing to death.

"Back," she whispered, turning and trying to fight her way through the snow, heading the way she'd just come. "Got to -"

Before she could get another word out, she stumbled and fell to her knees. The snow was up to her waist now, and when she tried to get up, she found that she could barely feel her legs. She took a moment to pull herself together, and she tried to focus on the fact that she simply had to find her car and head home; at the same time, she knew she'd been out walking through the forest for a few hours now, and the idea of spending a few hours again making her way back filled her with dread. She had no other options, however, so finally she reached out and grabbed the side of a nearby tree, using it to slowly haul herself up on legs that were on the verge of becoming numb.

"Got to go back," she murmured, as an icy wind blew against her face, burning her cheeks. "Got to..."

Her voice trailed off as her thoughts briefly

stopped. Realizing that she was on the brink of losing consciousness, she felt a rush of panic; she forced herself to keep going, stumbling through the snow for a couple of seconds before she once again lost all strength. Leaning against another tree, she realized that her body was trying to slide down into the snow, and she knew that if she let that happen, she'd most likely never get up again. Worried that she was beyond the point of no return but determined to keep going, she took a few more seconds to try to gather up every remaining scrap of energy.

"I'm not... I'm not going to die out here," she gasped, even as she felt the biting cold eating into her body. "I'm going to... find my way back... to the car."

"I knew this'd be how things ended for you," she heard her father saying. "You need to respect the power of the natural world, Lisa."

"I respect the... power of the natural world," she whispered, although her lips were starting to turn blue.

"Arrogance will get you nowhere."

"I'm not arrogant."

"You realize you might not ever be found if you die out here, right? By the time the snow thaws, you -"

"Shut up!" she hissed, turning to look over her shoulder as if she expected to see him. She saw nothing, of course, except more snow and trees, and after a few seconds she shook her head. "Idiot," she continued. "Stop being such an idiot, Lisa!"

She stepped forward again, feeling certain that she could at least manage a few steps, before immediately dropping to her knees again. This time she felt strangely dizzy, and when she tried to stand her legs seemed to be somehow frozen in place. She told herself that she needed another plan, and finally one popped into her dazed and delirious mind: she realized that everything would be alright if she just rested for a while, if she took a little sleep on the ground just for a few minutes. While a voice at the back of her mind was screaming that this would be a mistake, she was unable to stop herself as she began to settle down in the snow for a short nap.

"Just a few minutes," she whimpered as she felt the snow pressing against her face. "Just..."

Her voice trailed off again, and her eyes began to slip shut. For the next few seconds, curled on her side on the snow, Lisa allowed herself to start slipping away. Already, more snow was falling and starting to cover her, threatening to bury her entirely, but her mind was drifting off to a darker and warmer place. She let out a couple of faint murmurs, but after a moment the wind blew harder than ever, howling through the forest and forcing Lisa to open her eyes and sit up. Aware now that she'd been on the brink of death, she tried to get her breath back, taking in a series of short snatched gulps of air.

And then she saw it.

A light was burning nearby, breaking through the darkness. Somehow scrambling to her feet, with her father's old rifle slung over her shoulder, Lisa walked between the trees until she reached the edge of a clearing, and she blinked a few times in an attempt to clear her fading eyesight. The light was still burning, and over the next few seconds her blurred vision faded just enough to let her see that the light was in fact in the window of a small cabin. Not just any cabin, either.

This was the cabin she'd seen in her dreams. And as she stumbled out into the clearing, making her way toward the steps that led up to the cabin's front door, Lisa knew without a shadow of doubt that she'd been to this exact same place before. She just couldn't remember when, or how.

"Help me," she groaned, pushing through the snow as she tried to reach the front door. "Is there anyone here? Please... you have to help me!"

***

"No, I'm done here," Wade said as he shoved the last items into his backpack and began to fold it shut. "There's no point waiting until morning. I might as well hit the road."

"You're not too tired?" Karen asked over the phone.

"I can drive," he replied, before stopping for a moment as he saw the dirty sheets on the bed's other side. Just a few hours earlier, Lisa had been on those sheets, and the creases somehow reminded him of her presence. Reaching over, he touched the fabric but found that – as he should have guessed – all the warmth was gone now.

"Wade?" Karen said after a moment. "Are you still there?"

"Yeah, totally," he said, shocked by the fact that he was still thinking about Lisa so much. "Listen, I should get going. I need to check out, and I think there's a gas station at the edge of town that's open all night, so I should be able to grab a coffee. It's a really creepy little place, actually, it's right opposite a cemetery and -"

Stopping himself just in time, he looked at the doorway to the bathroom and remembered Lisa heading in there earlier. Again his heart felt swollen, as if part of him was yearning to see her again, but he told himself that he had to fight really hard and simply force those feelings away.

"Forget it," he continued as he felt tears gathering in his eyes. "Lisa, I love you and I'll be home tomorrow, okay?"

"Lisa?" Karen replied. "Did you just call me Lisa? Who's Lisa?"

"No-one," he stammered, horrified by his mistake. "Sorry, I've been watching the TV all night and I think I'm half out of my mind."

"I'm not sure you should be driving."

"I'll be fine, I promise," he told her. "You know me, I'm used to operating without much sleep. I love you, Karen, and I can't wait to get home and just hold you tight." He looked around the motel room for a moment. "I can't wait for this stage of my life to be over."

"Okay," she said cautiously, and the tone of her voice suggested that she wasn't entirely convinced. "Look after yourself, Wade. Sometimes I worry about you when you're on the road. You push yourself too hard."

"It's all to earn money for when the baby comes," he replied. "But this is the last trip." He looked at the empty bed again. "The very last trip. When I get home, I'll be staying home for good."

Once the call was over, he took a few minutes to finish gathering all his things. He knew deep down that part of him was playing a delaying game, that he was perhaps reluctant to leave Sobolton for the very last time. He briefly considered going to Lisa's place and saying goodbye again, but he knew that would be a risk too far; he wondered whether he should call her, but even that seemed dangerous. As he slipped his phone into his pocket, he told himself that he should simply delete her number and pick up a new phone when he got home, but somehow he was unable to quite contemplate such a drastic move. Instead he wondered whether he should send her one last message, just so that she'd know he cared.

Another tear rolled down his cheek.

"Just cut it off dead," he muttered as he once more saw the messy bed-sheets. "That's best for everyone."

He took a moment to wipe his eyes.

"Time to go," he whispered under his breath. "There's no -"

Before he could finish, he heard a gentle knock on the door. Turning, he saw that a figure was standing outside on the other side of the frosted glass, framed against the lights of the road as traffic raced past in the night. Already Wade could feel his heart racing, and as he headed to the door and pulled it open he couldn't help but hope that perhaps for some reason Lisa had returned. In fact, he couldn't think of any other possible explanation for the knock at all.

"Hey," he said as he opened the door. "I was just thinking about -"

He immediately froze as soon as he saw the figure standing outside. He'd been expecting Lisa, but instead Wade found himself staring at a man wearing a long dark coat. Opening his mouth to ask what the man wanted, and to suggest that he might have the wrong room, he suddenly realized that – even in the gloom – he could see thick patches of reddened skin all over the man's face, with the flesh criss-crossed by weltering patches that were clearly losing small flakes. The man looked red raw and sore all over.

"What -"

Before he could finish, the man grabbed him and pushed him into the room, quickly following and then slamming him into the wall. And then, before Wade had a chance to get another word out, the man grabbed him by the head and twisted hard, breaking his neck and letting his dead body slither down onto the dirty motel carpet. He landed in a crumpled heap at the man's feet.

CHAPTER THIRTY

Today...

"SUSAN WAS RIGHT," ROBERT said with a heavy weight in his voice, as he stepped back from setting the wreath down in front of the monument to the ten dead men. "There's almost nobody here."

Glancing around, John had to admit that this was true. Half a dozen people had shown up at the latest memorial event, and even those seemed to have been simply passing at the time. Already most of them were wandering off, leaving just John and Robert to contemplate the events that had taken place forty years earlier.

"I'd have thought," Robert continued, "that once you announced the recovery of the other three bodies, there might have been a little more interest.

God rest her soul, Susan would have hated to see such a low turnout. There were more people at her funeral. I don't want to sound like some cantankerous old bastard, John, but I can't help wondering why more people don't show a little respect for the past."

"Susan's funeral was very respectful," John told him. "I've been meaning to ask, how are you feeling after -"

"Oh, there's no need to get into that," Robert said, cutting him off. "She was a friend and I'll miss her. There's no more that needs saying." He cast a glance at John, as if to hammer home his point. "She was a good woman. I'd have thought the town would be buzzing with the news that those three men have finally been found."

"I rather think the news about the missing men was overshadowed by Joe's death," John pointed out.

"But you took the bones and skulls down, didn't you?"

"I did."

"Personally?"

"As it happens, yes," John replied. "They're sitting in a locker at the station awaiting formal identification, and then they'll be given a proper burial."

"And tell me something," Robert continued. "You don't strike me as the superstitious type, but when you took them down, did you cross the barrier at any point?"

John paused for a moment, not really sure how to explain.

"I took a ladder," he explained finally, clearly a little uncomfortable with the line of questioning.

"But did you cross the barrier? Did you go through the so-called gate?"

"Does that matter?"

"I don't know. Does it, John?"

"I honestly don't remember what I did," John told him, before pausing again. "Now that you mention it, though, I don't think I *did* cross the barrier. I didn't need to."

"You didn't, huh?"

"Didn't see the point." He paused, fully aware that Robert was still eyeing him with some combination of concern and amusement. "There's absolutely no need to read too much into that. Anyway, I was more interested in trying to find the microphones that must have been used to generate those voices. Unfortunately the site was briefly left unguarded, so they must have been taken away."

"People are muttering about Joe's death," Robert explained as the two of them turned and began to walk away from the memorial site. "It's not every day that a town's former sheriff gets attacked and more or less ripped apart by a pack of wild wolves, especially when officially there aren't supposed to be any wolves in the area at all."

"Did you know Lisa Sondnes?"

"I did," Robert admitted.

"She submitted a report to the station shortly before she disappeared," John explained. "Are there any local rumors about what happened to her?"

"There are not, to my knowledge," Robert muttered. "Which, in itself, is an odd thing. There are rumors about pretty much anything around these parts, but when Lisa vanished..."

His voice trailed off.

"I'm considering taking a look at that case again," John told him.

"Not got enough on your plate already?"

"It's a gut feeling," John said with a sigh. "I couldn't tell you why, but I can't shake the feeling that I could learn something important if I dig into the Lisa Sondnes case. I think perhaps it's because it's got Joe's fingerprints all over it. He didn't exactly pull out all the stops in an effort to find her. Don't you think that's suspicious?"

"A lot of what Joe did was suspicious."

"But this... I just need to dig a little. To be sure."

"Joe's wife was sick of the sight of him," Robert explained, "and I'd hazard a guess that she's quite glad he's gone, but she's still spreading rumors about his death. She's probably just hoping to drum up a little extra pension money now that she's a widow. I noticed your official report played up the idea that Joe died while helping to save Susan, and while locating the missing men. There wasn't so much in there about all the... other stuff."

"My report is intended as a statement of fact," John told him. "It's not the place for flights of fancy."

"So you still don't think that anything unusual happened out there?" Robert asked. "I respect that you don't believe in all that hocus pocus stuff, but I've got to wonder whether you have a breaking point."

"Everything that happened can be explained," John replied. "Joe's gun simply malfunctioned. The wolves must be strays that wandered into the area, and I've already called in a team to try to hunt them down. I don't know who put the bones up in the trees, but the world's not exactly short of lunatics and I'm sure I'll figure it out later."

"So everything strange can be explained, huh?"

"Yes, it can."

"And John," Robert continued, stopping at the edge of the sidewalk and turning to him, "don't get me wrong here, but you look like absolute shit."

"I'm sorry?"

"Have you had a single day off since you

started here in Sobolton?"

"I've not really had the chance," John pointed out. "There's still the dead girl to investigate, and plenty of paperwork concerning Wentworth Stone, and now all this business with the bodies in the forest and Joe's death. Not to mention Lisa Sondnes and a bunch of other cases."

"Everyone needs a day off," Robert told him. "You should know that as much as anyone. If you work yourself to the bone, you'll be less effective at your job. If you want to be a good sheriff round these parts, you absolutely need to keep yourself mentally and physically honed. And counter-intuitive as it might seem, taking a little time to rest is a big part of that."

"What are you suggesting I do?" John asked. "Take up a hobby? Start recreational drinking?"

"The weather's turning," Robert continued. "The snow's melting and there's no more coming, not this year. You live here long enough, you get a sense for that sort of thing. So I think, first thing tomorrow morning, you need to meet me outside the station." He turned and began to walk away. "I'm going to show you a different side of this place, John," he called out as he limped off along the sidewalk. "Prepare to have your mind well and truly blown!"

"Where are we going?" John asked, but he

quickly realized that Robert seemed not to be in much of a mood for explanations. "Robert? I'd like to at least know where we're going!"

"You'll see!" Robert shouted back at him. "Oh, and bring Tommy too! He's just as much in need of a break as you are!"

"But where are we going?" John continued plaintively, even though he knew he wasn't going to get an answer. After a moment he noticed that Robert was right; the snow *had* stopped falling, and some subtle change seemed to hint that spring was on its way. "Can you at least tell me where we're going? Robert? Where are you taking me tomorrow?"

***

"Fishing," Robert said the following morning, as he attached a lure to his line. "Call me sentimental, but I don't think there's an activity in this world that's better for a man's mind than fishing. It's like... golf for people with a sense of adventure."

"Do I put it on like this?" John asked, struggling a little with his own lure. "Is that right?"

"That's great," Robert replied, before looking a little further along the riverbank and seeing that Tommy was also making progress. "How are you doing there, young man? Are we ready?"

"I think so," Tommy stammered, clearly a little puzzled. "How does it look?"

"Great," Robert said with a smile. "And is your headache completely gone now?"

"It was a humdinger," Tommy admitted. "It lasted for days. I'm still not entirely sure what happened. Did I really say a load of strange stuff?"

Robert glanced at John, and for a moment they exchanged a knowing look.

"Enough of the shop talk," Robert replied, looking out across the river. "This is the absolute perfect time of year for fishing in these parts. I've been fishing for salmon all my life, and I happen to think that I've developed a kind of sixth sense for these things. As a lifelong bachelor, I've been blessed with plenty of time to indulge in my hobbies, and sometimes I think I can almost read the minds of these salmon as they swim past." He chuckled. "Don't worry, I don't *actually* believe that. Even for Sobolton, telepathic salmon might be a stretch too far. Then again, after what happened with those swans..."

"Sounds good to me," John muttered. "The fishing part, I mean."

"So you cast off like this," Robert explained, taking a moment to demonstrate before sitting down. "Now, there's one other thing you fellows need to know." He watched as they followed example, and then he waited until they were sitting next to him. "Men and women, in my limited experience, have very different ways of spending time together," he continued. "Women like to talk. They natter. They gossip. Now, I know I'm being old-fashioned and reductive, and I'm making great big sweeping generalizations that wouldn't really hold up to much scrutiny. But I don't care. Whereas men, in my – again, rather limited – experience, are much better suited to the silent pursuits."

"What's a silent pursuit?" Tommy asked.

"It's one where you don't feel the need to talk all the damn time," Robert replied with a faint grin. "Talking's overrated in my view, anyway. Silence is the greatest virtue of all. You know the seven deadly sins? I've always believed there should be an eighth, and that eighth sin should be verbosity."

"What does verbosity mean?" Tommy asked.

"Talking too much," John said firmly.

"That's exactly right," Robert added. "Silence should be prized. It should be practiced whenever possible." He watched the water for a moment. "If you talk all the time," he added finally, as if he was already losing his thoughts to the ripples on the water's surface, "you'll miss so very goddamn much that's going on in this world. And if you want me to add one last point, it'd be that all the great friendships I've had in my life have been ones that don't rely on words. The ability to be silent with someone is a true sign that you're getting things right." He paused for a moment. "Some people just don't know when to shut up."

"I think I might agree with you there," John admitted.

"Verbosity," Tommy muttered. "That's a new one on me."

"Big men don't fit in small houses," Robert said under his breath.

"What was that?" John asked.

"Gentlemen, the season is changing soon," Robert continued, leaning back in his camping chair as the river's water flowed gently past. "I for one think we should enjoy that change. Value it. Appreciate it. After all, none of us can be sure how many more seasons we're gonna get."

As their lures lay in wait beneath the water's surface, the three men sat on the riverbank and waited for the first hint that one of them might have caught something. All around them, the snow had finally stopped falling and the first signs of a thaw were showing through, with the land deeply engaged in the process of shifting from winter to spring. Water was dripping from various surfaces, encouraged by the sunshine that now bathed town and forest alike. On the riverbank, John sat with Robert and Tommy and watched the water, lost in thought as he contemplated the dead girl and the supposed gate in the forest and the strange case of Wentworth Stone – and also the case of missing veterinarian Lisa Sondnes, which was a niggling issue that he couldn't quite help thinking might in some way be connected. Meanwhile, high above, low clouds had cleared the tops of the mountains to the east of the town.

And for the next few hours, nobody said a word.

THE HORRORS OF SOBOLTON

1. Little Miss Dead
2. Swan Territory
3. Dead Widow Road
4. In a Lonely Grave
5. Electrification
6. Man on the Moon

More titles coming soon!

Next in this series

IN A LONELY GRAVE
(THE HORRORS OF SOBOLTON BOOK 4)

Out in the forest, beyond the edge of town, there's a place where nobody goes. According to legend, a strange creature lives deep in the darkness, trapped in a pit as it waits for its next victim. Some say the creature is real, others claim that it was real once but died many years ago.

Sheriff John Tench is about to uncover the shocking truth.

As he continues his investigation into the case of the dead girl, John finds himself drawn into an ancient mystery. Face to face with unspeakable evil, he soon realizes that one of Sobolton's most terrifying legends is rooted in a tragedy that struck the town years ago. But can he end this tragedy after so many years, or is the pain destined to repeat for generations to come?

Meanwhile Lisa starts to notice strange discrepancies in her life, leading her to question whether everything she sees can be real.

Also by Amy Cross

1689
(The Haunting of Hadlow House book 1)

All Richard Hadlow wants is a happy family and a peaceful home. Having built the perfect house deep in the Kent countryside, now all he needs is a wife. He's about to discover, however, that even the most perfectly-laid plans can go horribly and tragically wrong.

The year is 1689 and England is in the grip of turmoil. A pretender is trying to take the throne, but Richard has no interest in the affairs of his country. He only cares about finding the perfect wife and giving her a perfect life. But someone – or something – at his newly-built house has other ideas. Is Richard's new life about to be destroyed forever?

Hadlow House is brand new, but already there are strange whispers in the corridors and unexplained noises at night. Has Richard been unlucky, is his new wife simply imagining things, or is a dark secret from the past about to rise up and deliver Richard's worst nightmare? Who wins when the past and the present collide?

AMY CROSS

Also by Amy Cross

The Haunting of Nelson Street
(The Ghosts of Crowford book 1)

Crowford, a sleepy coastal town in the south of England, might seem like an oasis of calm and tranquility. Beneath the surface, however, dark secrets are waiting to claim fresh victims, and ghostly figures plot revenge.

Having finally decided to leave the hustle of London, Daisy and Richard Johnson buy two houses on Nelson Street, a picturesque street in the center of Crowford. One house is perfect and ready to move into, while the other is a fire-ravaged wreck that needs a lot of work. They figure they have plenty of time to work on the damaged house while Daisy recovers from a traumatic event.

Soon, they discover that the two houses share a common link to the past. Something awful once happened on Nelson Street, something that shook the town to its core.

Also by Amy Cross

The Revenge of the Mercy Belle
(The Ghosts of Crowford book 2)

The year is 1950, and a great tragedy has struck the town of Crowford. Three local men have been killed in a storm, after their fishing boat the Mercy Belle sank. A mysterious fourth man, however, was rescue. Nobody knows who he is, or what he was doing on the Mercy Belle... and the man has lost his memory.

Five years later, messages from the dead warn of impending doom for Crowford. The ghosts of the Mercy Belle's crew demand revenge, and the whole town is being punished. The fourth man still has no memory of his previous existence, but he's married now and living under the named Edward Smith. As Crowford's suffering continues, the locals begin to turn against him.

What really happened on the night the Mercy Belle sank? Did the fourth man cause the tragedy? And will Crowford survive if this man is not sent to meet his fate?

Also by Amy Cross

**The Devil, the Witch and the Whore
(The Deal book 1)**

"Leave the forest alone. Whatever's out there, just let it be. Don't make it angry."

When a horrific discovery is made at the edge of town, Sheriff James Kopperud realizes the answers he seeks might be waiting beyond in the vast forest. But everybody in the town of Deal knows that there's something out there in the forest, something that should never be disturbed. A deal was made long ago, a deal that was supposed to keep the town safe. And if he insists on investigating the murder of a local girl, James is going to have to break that deal and head out into the wilderness.

Meanwhile, James has no idea that his estranged daughter Ramsey has returned to town. Ramsey is running from something, and she thinks she can find safety in the vast tunnel system that runs beneath the forest. Before long, however, Ramsey finds herself coming face to face with creatures that hide in the shadows. One of these creatures is known as the devil, and another is known as the witch. They're both waiting for the whore to arrive, but for very different reasons. And soon Ramsey is offered a terrible deal, one that could save or destroy the entire town, and maybe even the world.

AMY CROSS

Also by Amy Cross

The Soul Auction

"I saw a woman on the beach. I watched her face a demon."

Thirty years after her mother's death, Alice Ashcroft is drawn back to the coastal English town of Curridge. Somebody in Curridge has been reviewing Alice's novels online, and in those reviews there have been tantalizing hints at a hidden truth. A truth that seems to be linked to her dead mother.

"Thirty years ago, there was a soul auction."

Once she reaches Curridge, Alice finds strange things happening all around her. Something attacks her car. A figure watches her on the beach at night. And when she tries to find the person who has been reviewing her books, she makes a horrific discovery.

What really happened to Alice's mother thirty years ago? Who was she talking to, just moments before dropping dead on the beach? What caused a huge rockfall that nearly tore a nearby cliff-face in half? And what sinister presence is lurking in the grounds of the local church?

Also by Amy Cross

The Haunting of Hurst House
(Mercy Willow book 1)

When she moves to a small coastal Cornish village, Mercy Willow hopes to start a new life. She has a brand new job as an estate agent, and she's determined to put the past where it belongs and get on with building a new future. But will that be easy in a village that has more than its fair share of ghosts?

Determined to sell the un-sellable Hurst House, Mercy gets straight to work. Hurst House was once the scene of a terrible tragedy, and many of the locals believe that the place is best left untouched and undisturbed. Mercy, however, thinks it just needs a lick of paint and a few other improvements, and that then she'll be able to find a buyer in no time.

Soon, Mercy discovers that parts of Hurst House's past are still lingering. Strange noises hint at an unseen presence, and an old family secret is about to come bursting back to life with terrifying consequences. Meanwhile, Mercy herself has a dark past that she'd rather keep hidden. After all, her name isn't really Mercy Willow at all, and she's running from something that has already almost killed her once.

AMY CROSS

Also by Amy Cross

The Ghost of Molly Holt

"Molly Holt is dead. There's nothing to fear in this house."

When three teenagers set out to explore an abandoned house in the middle of a forest, they think they've found the location where the infamous Molly Holt video was filmed.

They've found much more than that...

Tim doesn't believe in ghosts, but he has a crush on a girl who does. That's why he ends up taking her out to the house, and it's also why he lets her take his only flashlight. But as they explore the house together, Tim and Becky start to realize that something else might be lurking in the shadows.

Something that, ten years ago, suffered unimaginable pain.

Something that won't rest until a terrible wrong has been put right.

Also by Amy Cross

American Coven

He kidnapped three women and held them in his basement. He thought they couldn't fight back. He was wrong...

Snatched from the street near her home, Holly Carter is taken to a rural house and thrown down into a stone basement. She meets two other women who have also been kidnapped, and soon Holly learns about the horrific rituals that take place in the house. Eventually, she's called upstairs to take her place in the ice bath.

As her nightmare continues, however, Holly learns about a mysterious power that exists in the basement, and which the three women might be able to harness. When they finally manage to get through the metal door, however, the women have no idea that their fight for freedom is going to stretch out for more than a decade, or that it will culminate in a final, devastating demonstration of their new-found powers.

Also by Amy Cross

The Ash House

Why would anyone ever return to a haunted house?

For Diane Mercer the answer is simple. She's dying of cancer, and she wants to know once and for all whether ghosts are real.

Heading home with her young son, Diane is determined to find out whether the stories are real. After all, everyone else claimed to see and hear strange things in the house over the years. Everyone except Diane had some kind of experience in the house, or in the little ash house in the yard.

As Diane explores the house where she grew up, however, her son is exploring the yard and the forest. And while his mother might be struggling to come to terms with her own impending death, Daniel Mercer is puzzled by fleeting appearances of a strange little girl who seems drawn to the ash house, and by strange, rasping coughs that he keeps hearing at night.

The Ash House is a horror novel about a woman who desperately wants to know what will happen to her when she dies, and about a boy who uncovers the shocking truth about a young girl's murder.

AMY CROSS

AMY CROSS

BOOKS BY AMY CROSS

AMY CROSS

For more information, visit:

www.amycross.com

AMY CROSS

Printed in Great Britain
by Amazon

39232423R00169